JOHN RECHY

PABLO!

Arte Público Press
Houston, Texas

Pablo! is funded in part by grants from the City of Houston through the Houston Arts Alliance and the National Endowment for the Arts. We are grateful for their support.

Recovering the past, creating the future

Arte Público Press
University of Houston
4902 Gulf Fwy, Bldg 19, Rm 100
Houston, Texas 77204-2004

Cover design by Victoria Castillo

Names: Rechy, John, author.
Title: Pablo! : a novel / by John Rechy.
Description: Houston, TX : Arte Publico Press, [2018]
Identifiers: LCCN 2017061346 (print) | LCCN 2018003499
    (ebook) | ISBN 9781518504877 (epub) | ISBN 9781518504884
    (kindle) | ISBN 9781518504891 (pdf) | ISBN 9781558858602
    (softcover : acid-free paper)
Subjects: | GSAFD: Allegories.
Classification: LCC PS3568.E28 (ebook) | LCC PS3568.E28 P37
    2018 (print) | DDC 813/.54—dc23
LC record available at https://lccn.loc.gov/2017061346

♾ The paper used in this publication meets the requirements of the American National Standard for Information Sciences—Permanence of Paper for Printed Library Materials, ANSI Z39.48-1984.

3 1969 02642 2831

18 19 20 21   5 4 3 2 1

TABLE OF CONTENTS

ACKNOWLEDGEMENTS

Thanks to Professor Francisco A. Lomelí for his illuminating footnotes and Afterword and major role in bringing this book out of archival retirement.

Thanks to Felix Franquiz for his dedication in restoring illegible inked passages in the original manuscript into printable form.

Thanks to John Bates for transforming a frail Royal-portable-typed manuscript into its new format.

Thanks to Georges Borchardt for his encouraging enthusiasm and professional counsel.

Thanks to Professor Nicolás Kanellos for guidance toward the publication of this book.

Thanks to Wilford Leach, in memoriam, the first to read this book in manuscript and the first to believe in it and me.

And, as always, thanks to Michael Ewing for his support and astute creative observations and suggestions, and for his years-long determination to bring this book to publication. Without such dedication, this book would not exist.

Brief sections of this book, in different form, have appeared in "Bachy" and the *Los Angeles Book Review.*

For my mother,
Guadalupe Flores Rechy

PABLO!

And the soul must wander
aimlessly until the sun and
the moon shall fuse.

     —Mayan Legend

THE PAST: The Village

ONE: The Girl, the Man and the Woman

1

"It is the Xtabay."

The old man squinted to see through the rain.

"It is the Xtabay," repeated the frightened voice of his wife huddled behind him. "It is she who lures men with her unholy beauty." She crossed herself and recited a prayer, unaware of the rain wetting her.

And her memory sang the words of the evil Xtabay, and she could almost hear the illusive voice calling like music played by the wind on trees,

"*Tuux ca bin?*

Coten uayé . . ."

beckoning the old man to come to her, luring him as she had lured others to their death,

"Where are you going?

Come with me. . . ."

"It is only a girl who is lost and has fainted," said the old man. "It is not an evil spirit. I would feel it." For once in a village far away he had been a holy man, and he was warned of evil as others are warned of rain. "We must help her."

"She is pretending sleep to lure you." The woman's voice was hardly audible over the rain. "Say a prayer and leave her," the old woman demanded. The sharp claws of her ancient hands would not release her husband's arm.

And as the man proceeded toward the form of the girl encompassed by the fantastic green of the plants, he mumbled something and crossed himself.

The old woman remained behind, clasping her bony hands. From the distance she saw her husband kneel before the girl, and fear enveloped her like a shroud. She took a step forward. The earth would open and swallow the man. She would hear the wicked laughter of the Xtabay, then the mocking song mingling with the sound of the rain.

But none of this happened. She saw, instead, the old man lift the girl in his arms, saw him walk back with her, still asleep or fainted deceptively, pretending whichever she wanted.

"She has fainted from exhaustion," said the man as he approached the livid old woman trembling with religious fear.

"No," said the woman, moving back frantically as the body was brought closer to her. "You do not understand. Her beauty hides evil." As she moved farther back, she watched the face of the girl in fascination, and she understood why men were lured so easily to their destruction. This young girl in her husband's arms, evil as she was, was as beautiful as the flower of the Tzacam, into which she converted herself after bringing unholy death to men.

"If it were the Xtabay, I would feel it in my heart," said the man who in a village far away had been a holy man.

"But the face—the body," persisted the woman in an awed whisper, "they could destroy even a holy man such as you."

The man walked into the house with the girl. The wife followed a distance behind.

Inside, the sound of the rain was unreal, ominous, and the woman crossed herself again as she hurried to the corner of the one room, where the live skeleton of an ancient woman shrouded with brown skin crouched. It was the mother of the wife.

The man laid the girl gently in the hammock.

"She is very wet," he said solemnly to his wife. "Take her clothes."

The woman only retreated farther into the corner, cringing on the floor beside the fading skeleton shrouded in the horrible brown skin, thin enough that the bones were visible. And they were stark and white. The wife clung to her mother, pressing herself against the disintegrating body, clasping at the torn clothes, so that the two old women were like desiccated eagles feeding on each other.

"He has brought the evil woman into this house," the man's wife whispered to the skeleton of her mother. "He has brought the Xtabay inside."

The mother stared fixedly before her. Her eyes were covered by a thin white mist, and she never blinked. She heard only one word through the vortex of her time-destroyed mind, and that word whirled around and around, and it echoed, "Xtabay." She would have raised one terrified trembling hand, but her mind stopped thinking and she remained silent.

When the man saw that his wife would not come, he began to remove the girl's clothes. He stopped abruptly, turning away. The ancient hand touched the smooth flesh of the girl's arm. Quickly, he withdrew it. He gazed at the face, at the closed eyes, the black hair moist on her face. He turned away fiercely.

On the hammock, the girl was breathing audibly. She could hear the soft rain even in the stupor into which she had fallen. She heard the thunder, once, and it burst loudly in her mind and then entered the realm of silence. She spun toward unconsciousness, into the world of pure motion.

"Look, he is lost, he cannot move, she has paralyzed him, he is lost to the evil Xtabay." The wife's voice rose hysterical and insane. She embraced the skin-shrouded skeleton beside her.

Once again, the name reverberated in the mother's ears, and, her mind clinging to the word this time, she began to chant from the wasteland of her memory the legend of the Xtabay, to chant like a priest the words long buried in her mind, confusing her own life with the life of the other, the lonely hunter of her tale.

"She who lures all men . . . searching until time ends for physical love—searching in death because in life she denied the spiritual . . . to fill her empty yearning." She chuckled mirthlessly. "Lost . . . " she breathed. "Lost searching a substitute for salvation. . . . " Then she trembled, as if completely alive again. "And I became a flower full of thorns . . . . But the Xkeban, my sister, who loved in life, smells of beauty."

The old man retreated from the hammock, and in a moment he returned to cover the girl's body. He who was a holy man, who was very, very old—and closer now to the spirits and the great god, he who had even denied his wife to remain pure—he had almost surrendered to the evil of desire.

"And the man saw her standing at the door, and he let her in, for it was raining," the wheezing voice of the mother continued. "My father, who is dead, the Xtabay lied . . . but he did not believe her, for he recognized the luring, sweet voice of evil. . . . For all evil is sweet. . . . And as he held me in life—before my wandering death—I strained to reach his young body, not his soul, and then it came to me like a god. . . . And he burned a strand of her hair and buried the ashes, to keep the evil from him. . . . "

For the first time, the wife became aware of the mother's voice. And remembering the ancient charm, she stared at the girl's long hair.

The girl opened her eyes. She felt the woman's hatred. But she closed her eyes again quickly because this was the world of reality, of unrealized desire.

"You are lost," the old man told her softly, crushing the evil within him. "And I will help you find your way, wherever it is."

She opened her mouth, concentrating on the words she must form. Finally she was able to whisper, "To the modern city of the Mexican people. . . . "

And in that instant she saw lightning lash at the sky, and the lightning became the lithe, supple whirling body of a boy of desperate eyes. She called for him. Then there was no lightning, and the turbulent body was gone.

When the old man was certain that the girl would speak no more, he went to his wife, his head lowered. The memory of the sin still scorched him. He must vindicate himself, he was too close to god.

"When the girl wakes," he told his wife, whose face was contorted by fear, "I will take her wherever she will want to go."

His wife shrieked unintelligibly at him as she clung to the stark-white bones of her mother.

On this side of the house, the ground was moist but dry enough to sustain a fire, for the rain fell lightly and obliquely. The wife of the man who in a far-away village had been holy stood looking down at the ground, her fists clenched.

In one hand, she held something black.

She knelt on the ground, laying beside her what she had held in her fist. It was a long strand of the girl's hair. The old woman dug into the earth with her hands, and triumph was written on the hollow-cheeked face. When she had finished digging, she made a fire on the ground, and ceremoniously, aware of her affinity to good, she burned the girl's hair. In a moment there was nothing left but a small pinch of ashes. She collected them carefully and dropped them into the hole, covering it quickly.

As she walked into the thatched house, the claws of her hands were buried into her flesh, cutting.

2

In a village far away, the father of the girl stared at the clouded sky. The rain fell in scattered drops.

About him, in the surrounding *milpas*[1] a distance away where the corn would be grown, smoke rose in gray clouds. The other villagers had banded together, rushing from field to field to burn the brush that must be burned before the planting of the maize. But the father of the girl was alone. And it was perhaps too late to fire the brush in his field—had been too late even as he had stood at the entrance to the village returning to his house to find his daughter gone.

Like the others, he had watched the skies daily for a sign, and he had watched the brush, still green, knowing that he must wait until it was dry enough to burn. Now the rain had come unexpectedly, and the long hours in the field cutting the brush, digging with his bare hands for the ground-clutching roots, would be wasted.

From a distance very far—above the sound of the burning brush, the cracking fire struggling against the erratic rain, over the sound of stamping feet of men rushing with flaming *tahche*[2] in hand—the man heard the words of supplication to the ancient deities of the field and the mysterious Catholic god, and he heard the doleful voice of one of the elders of the village forming the words almost forgotten by a new generation of *milperos*,[3]

---

[1]Corn fields.
[2]A long stick used to light the brush.
[3]Men who work the corn fields.

*"Cu yantal in kubic le zaca ti nohol ik yetel ti
kakal-mozon-kanik. . . . "*
"To the south wind and the furious whirling wind, I
offer this *zaca*.[4] . . . "
Now the trembling hand would be thrusting the corn into
the air, that suddenly the rain would stop and the friendly wind
would blow across the land carrying the fire across the fields, all
this before the storm came smothering the fire and soaking the
bushes, rendering the fields useless for the planting.
"To the east wind also, so to the four corners of my
field. . . . "
The father of the girl stood like one dead with open eyes,
and the only sign of life was the perspiration that covered his
face, his arms, his legs. But he did not feel this, or the steamy
heat. He felt only the sadness of the impending ruin of his field
and the greater loss of his daughter.
"To the north, to the west, to the south winds also,
so to the great god father and the sainted lord
archangel. . . . "
And standing so, aware of the crushing power of something
which he hated and could not understand, he seemed to have
sprung from the soil. His face was dark brown-red, like the land
itself, and like the land it was harsh, strong, And that harsh
strength shone in every part of him. His hair was dark, black, as
were his fierce eyes, and his body was powerful, with muscles
sharply carved by streaks of perspiration.
"In the name of god the father, of god the son, of god the
holy ghost, amen," ended the lugubrious chant of the elder.
And the rain stopped.
And the father of the girl who was gone looked up into the
sky, very long, and then, with resuscitated hope, he was running

---

[4]A leather bag used for bailing.

swiftly toward his own field, the tahche in his hand—the long stick to fire the brush. He ran unstopping for a long time, and then he was standing in his field. At various places his legs were cut with the thorny plants of this country.

The ground about him was unhallowed, and pleasure surged through him at the realization, and he breathed furiously. No holy *h-menob*[5] had prayed over it, no altar had been erected to the field gods, no *zaca* offered to the spirits of his *milpa*. He had defied the spirits, the holy *chaacs* and *balams*,[6] and the rain had stopped, and he could win again, could still burn the brush. Life pounded violently in him, as it had earlier, the months before when he had searched greedily for the fertile land, where the palms heralded the excellence of this soil, surged through him as it had when he had cleared the land, attacking each tree with the small ax as if he were slaying the spirits of the ancient gods whom he hated, digging out the roots, ripping the earth, attacking nature and defying the god.

The raised *tahche* in his hand was flaming, and he was running across the field. The fire passed from the pole of *catzim* wood to the crying trees and bushes. Smoke ascended. The wood began to sputter, and then to crack, and then the fire came alive, roaring, and the flames whirled open-jawed and embraced the land.

And then the sky burst open, and the rain came pouring. It fell over the fire, hissing, soaking the scorched earth, the brush, and very soon the flames were gone, and only the mocking sight of smoke remained.

---

[5]Holy men.

[6]A *chaac* is a rock figure that dots many Mayan ruins, consisting of a man figure lying down on his back with a sacrificial or ritual disk on his stomach. A *balam* is a supernatural being in Mayan religion that guards corn fields and villages.

And the rain released the heat of the soil that rose like a judgment in furious waves of steam.

The house of the man was farther from the others than is usual. It was like all the others, of poles interlacing, of mud plaster, of green covering.

The father of the girl saw the house, and he thought of the woman who would be inside, and he thought of his field, soaked useless.

He walked into the house.

The rain had entered at various places. Streaks of dark light lined the floor and spilled into the water that had gathered. It was almost barren, this house of the one room, like the others in the village. From the ceiling the paten hung dismally, now wet, in which the food was kept. Against the walls were the metate[7] for the grinding of the maize, and the baskets, the small bench, the hammock. . . .

He turned away quickly from the hammock. But his eyes returned involuntarily. And as if the memory had buried a knife in his heart, he remembered the girl who was gone.

Urgently, he turned to face his wife.

3

She knelt facing him on the floor, the hands lying one on the other as if she had been praying. The face was solemn. The skin over the skull seemed so tight that laughter appeared impossible, as if it would rend the skin. It was a thin face, inscrutable, secret.

---

[7]A stone, usually volcanic, used to grind corn and other vegetables and spices.

It was only the eyes that gave her life—long and slanted and very, very deep. It was they that showed emotion, and they laughed now triumphantly.

Her hair was braided tightly into one braid that coiled like a thick snake at the nape of her neck. She was dressed in immaculate white, which clung to her slim body. Her feet were bare.

The man stared at his wife, into the abysmal eyes.

The eyes burst into greater laughter. They mocked, boasted of her triumph and of his defeat, soundless laughter quivered on her lips. The face was solemn.

Anger seared him. Her eyes were a mirror of the past months, and he saw himself under the blazing sky digging into the earth. Desperately, he turned away from her and sought again the empty hammock. Again, he faced the woman. He stood over her, his body so tense that his legs began to bleed from the thorny cuts.

He pulled her up with both hands. He shook her so violently by the shoulders that the braided snake coiled at her neck unwound its body and hung limply the length of her back.

"Laugh," he shouted.

But the face did not move. It remained a mask which only tearing can change.

He slapped the mask, to remove it, trying to make the face cry. The despised eyes laughed and boasted.

She fell to the ground, at his feet. She looked up at him. Silent laughter quivered on her lips. The mask was impassive.

Standing over her, he shouted, "You have been praying . . . for this."

The strange eyes smiled.

"And you won," he said dully.

"They won," she said.

"Your gods," he said.

The eyes laughed.

"And the field is destroyed . . . lost . . . months, long, long months," he said. "And the girl . . . she is gone too. Forever."

"I have prayed," she said softly. "I have prayed for the destruction of your field. And I have prayed for the boy that has taken her from you. And now there will be vindication for the sin."

Helpless fury flashed through him, helpless because no matter what he did she was the victor. "And even as I was in the field, even as the sun burned . . . Even then, you were praying."

"Yes," she said.

Anger burst into passion, lust and hatred becoming one, both demanding gratification. He longed to conquer her, to hurt and destroy her, as she had destroyed him. And yet he longed even more to make her a part of him, to dispel in that way the unbearable loneliness inside him, to make her feel the loss as he felt it, to make her understand as he understood.

His breath came in spasms now, and something beat in his head louder than the rain outside. He knelt before the woman. He put his hands gently inside the immaculate dress, drawing it easily from her breasts.

She did not move.

He called her name softly, with something more than tenderness, something which not only demanded but pled urgently. Still, she did not respond, and his hands moved over her body.

"I want you," came his choked words. "I want you, like on that night, so long ago. . . . "

"No," she whispered quickly, and there was the barest echo of emotion in her voice, and the face seemed alive. But the mask covered it again, and the stoical voice said, "She is gone now, gone forever now to seek the boy."

"I want you," he repeated.

"My body."

His arms were wet, his whole body was wet with the rain and the perspiration as he raised her in his arms. He felt himself bursting with power, and his fingers dug into her flesh as he had dug for the roots in the ripped earth of his field. He placed her on the ground and knelt over her.

And as he took her fiercely, she remained like one long dead.

TWO: The Girl

1

The girl still lay in the hammock of the holy man.

Her eyes were closed, but she was not asleep. She turned with a moan, licking the perspiration thirstily from her lips. She opened her mouth to ask for water, but no sound came, and she sighed and turned her head toward the window beyond which the rain fell in sad streaks from the darkening sky.

Huddled on the ground at the far side of the room, the wife of the holy man sat. The room was unbearably hot, the air thick and moist, but fear made the old woman cold, and she covered herself with a shroud. Her eyes were fixed intently on the girl, and she watched anxiously for her breathing, which was harsh and irregular, and the old woman was thinking, *She is still breathing, but it will soon stop—all movement, all life, will soon stop.* She smiled, clinging to a rosary in her hands.

Apprehensively, she searched for her husband, and she saw him sitting a few feet from the girl, his hands over his forehead.

The woman's mother slept grotesquely beside her with fixed open eyes, tiny and ugly and wrinkled like an unborn child.

The wife of the man fixed her gaze again on the girl. *We will be free of the evil,* she thought. *And the man would once again be holy, as in that village far away, and there would be peace once again.*

And she thought of the black hair lying in ashes in the tiny hole outside. She tightened her fingers about the rosary. She was remembering the story of the man who had sheltered the Xtabay, remembering from childhood the man who had believed the evil one's tale that her father was dead, that the Xkeban, her sister, had sent her jealously from the house. As she remembered this, she expected with undeviating belief to see the girl on the hammock disappear into memory.

The girl turned. The man stood over her. She saw the blurred ancient face. He touched her forehead, and it was hot and feverish.

"She is burning with fever," he told his wife.

But the old woman only smiled secretly, and she thought, *Yes, she is burning, and the evil is burning too.*

"Please . . . " the girl muttered, but she could say no more, and she licked her lips feeling the perspiration touch her tongue.

The man's wife stood. The shroud fell from her shoulders, very black like the girl's hair. She watched the girl, smiling secretly, her long wrinkled fingers feeling the tiny head of the crucified Christ on her rosary.

The man brought the girl water. He neared the clay cup to her lips, and she raised her head with much effort. But before the water could touch her parched mouth, she fell back with a long harsh groan.

The man's wife approached the hammock cautiously like a vulture nearing the almost-dead. The tiny beads of the rosary were clenched tightly in her wrinkled hands. She searched the young face. It was death-pale, motionless.

"She is dead," the woman cried. "The Xtabay is dead, I have killed her. The evil is dead."

But she recoiled in anger like an ancient bird denied prey when she saw that the girl on the hammock was still breathing.

The girl was aware of herself lying on the hammock. She was aware of the intense heat, and of the old man and the woman whom she did not know. Even in the dimness of almost-night she could see through the window the endless green of the brushy country converging with the dark horizon, could see the sad rain. Still it was as if she had entered the realm of another world, unreal outside of herself.

And this world was one of pure notion, whirling, voluptuous, turning. In her mind, someone was dancing frenziedly. A boy. The boy of the lithe, supple, young body. He took form, then disappeared quickly. Only the frenzy of the dancing remained. There was no dancer, no boy. Only motion. And it became a world of pure sound for the girl—strange sound which occasionally was silence.

The world outside of herself was one of heat and rain-pouring clouds and green country fusing with gray sky. But the world within was one of sweet motion and sound. Even as she tried to surrender to the world inside, the world of the whirling motions and silent sound, the world of the lost boy, she felt thirsty, and again the heat embraced her, and this was the world of reality.

She turned toward the window, hoping that the rain would come pouring through the roof, on her face, into her mouth, drenching her body.

At that moment the old man held the cup of water to her lips again, and she drank anxiously. Her hands reached for the hammock as she felt herself spin dizzily into unconsciousness, into that world of pure motion and sound, the world of the past, and of the boy, the world of unrealized desire.

2

I, the girl.

If I could speak, if I could mold the feelings into words, if I could bring forth the heart, if I could shape the pain, the longing, the loneliness, the long-sought love, if I could hold the heart naked in my hands, if I could let it beat the words, the hidden knowledge, the buried secrets.

If I could speak . . .

What would I tell?

That in memory, and even beyond memory, there is this.

The woman stood enveloped in the greenness of the rain-pleading earth. Her face burned angrily in the furious sun, which radiated waves of relentless animate heat.

Behind her were the small thatch houses of the village as she began to run, barefooted, across the thorny land, feeling the child in her womb twist painfully and grasp for her flesh.

She fell to the ground. Knife-pointed plants stabbed her body, but her strength was gone and she could not move. She lay on the fuming ground, and her perspiration and her tears were swallowed greedily by the thirsty earth. The sun fell full on her face as she pressed herself against the earth, hoping to feel the child inside her die.

At last, the white sun yellowed, almost touching the horizon, and then it spilled orange across the land, and there were clouds ready to receive it as it fell bringing night. And the bowl of sky was dark. One star appeared in the inverted sea, and the star was frozen.

Night had come like a woman mourning death.

And feeling the night enshroud her, the woman thought, *The day has died and the child within me is still alive.*

A noise broke the silence, and the woman struggled to rise, but she could not, and she listened intently, frightened, remembering the tales of wandering spirits, of the head which sought its body in the night, of animals possessed by unresting souls. Her lips moved soundlessly. She could not even pray now.

The brush rustled again. Her eyes strained to pierce the darkness.

A deer stood nearby. Then there was another rustling, and a smaller deer appeared next to the first. Both stood as if looking at the woman. The smaller deer leaned against the larger.

Mother and child, the woman thought as she felt the unborn child twist within her, so painfully that she buried her finger-nails into the ground. The elbow upon which she had propped herself twisted, and her face fell to the dirt. The woman laughed until tears came. The laughter choked, and she screamed biting her hand until she could taste blood.

She awoke to the sound of voices. A bright light burned over her, the light of a burning *tahche*. She stared into the flame not understanding until she heard the muffled voice of a man, her F. He knelt beside her and touched her forehead.

There was another voice, the voice of an older woman.

Three other men hovered over her like birds. The burning light illuminated only their faces, and they were like bodiless heads swimming in darkness. The light cast fantastic shadows as the flames swayed, and it seemed to the woman on the ground that all about her were staggering drunkenly ready to fall. There was the buzzing of voices.

"Are they gone?" the woman on the ground whispered.

"We are still here," said the voice of a man not her husband. The man who had spoken stood over her with his hands on his breast as if she was already dead. "We have come to help you."

The husband did not speak. He held his wife's hand. He could feel it hot and moist.

"Are they gone?" she demanded harshly.

"We are still here," the voice repeated.

"No," whispered the woman weakly. "Not you. The deer. Two deer."

The older woman stepped from the group of faces. She leaned her ear against the woman's stomach.

One of the men crossed himself and began to pray softly. Soon, all the men were kneeling, except the husband, who suddenly stood up. And the others began to pray.

"Dios te salve, reina y madre . . . "[8]

The dark threatened to smother the light of the flaming stick. The husband's lips did not move, did not pray, and he did not kneel. He stood defiantly holding the flaming stick and staring into the impenetrable sky, hearing his wife moan.

"Is the child dead?" he asked the older woman finally.

"I cannot hear," said the older woman, pressing her ear more closely against the other's stomach.

The men stopped praying momentarily, and then they resumed more softly, beating their chests religiously with tightened fists.

"Vuelve a nosotros esos tus ojos . . . "[9]

Crossing herself and sighing, the older woman said to the husband, "It is alive, she has not killed your child."

The woman on the ground opened her eyes. "Oh, god," she sighed feebly. "Still, the growing sin . . . Oh, god, god." Then she fainted.

The man dropped the pole of *catzim* wood. He lifted his wife in his arms. For a moment, he stood looking deep into the blackened face, his arms tight about her. He brought his head against her breast, crying.

"Why?" he whispered.

---

[8]May God save you, queen and mother. . .
[9]Return to us, your eyes . . .

The light of the fallen *tahche* faded. The night caved in upon them. They stood in the blackness. The men began to chant very softly again the prayers of the new people.

"*Ruega por nosotros los pecadores ahora y en la hora de nuestra muerte . . .* "[10]

3

I, the girl.
What would I tell?
This.

And that woman writhing with pain was my mother, and I was the child forming in her womb, and that man was my father, and she tried to kill me before I was born. (But that is beyond memory, and this I do not know, and so if I remember, it is not conscious remembering, and if I speak, it is not conscious speaking)and the house was away from those of the others living in the village, so that I grew alone, and when I was a child the women would pass our house going to the *milpas* of their husbands taking their food, but I did not speak to them because they were afraid of us although I can remember that once there was a woman who held me in her arms and said I would be her daughter, until my father heard her and he tore me from her and he shouted that I was his and I never went to that other woman, and the woman who was my mother did not speak and she prayed daily to the mysterious spirits, and daily she went to the church, where I entered once, alone, seeing the strange dolls that seemed so sad, the small one in a niche where many candles burned, the strange black-draped doll which was so wondrous that I reached for it and held it in my arms, and I sat on one of

---

[10]Pray for us sinners now and at the hour of our death . . .

the small wooden benches before which the sad man with the thorns on his head and arms stretched on the cross, wept, and over and over I rocked the doll in my arms . . . until the woman who was my mother came all in black with her face covered with a veil falling to her feet, which were always bare, and she knelt at the door without yet seeing me, clenching her hands in prayer, kneeling on the dirt floor, moving forward on her knees, until she reached the place where the sad man was nailed to the cross, and she kissed the cloth at his feet, and looking at her, I realized she was beautiful too, like the doll in my arms, and I walked to where she knelt, and she looked at me as if not recognizing me, that woman who never spoke to me, who never touched me, staring at me until she recognized me, until she gave a long cry like that of a bird I had seen dying in the field of my father, and she snatched the doll from my arms, and the doll of the sad painted face fell to the ground, so hard that its head broke off, while beside me the woman who is my mother moved away clenching the black veil as if to shelter herself from me, and then again she was at the door, but as I approached her again, I heard her saying this—which I did not understand—Why do you pursue me in the form of that child, why does evil follow me forever, is there no vindication? And when she had finished she was not speaking to me but to the sky, which was very white, until the dark came, until the moon came, until I went, still a child, still not knowing, to the *milpa* of my father where he went to guard the field from the animals that wandered in the night, who were, he told me, the souls of the restless dead, and he would hold me in his arms and shelter me from the night and speak to me in a voice which I loved, so that once I said you are my father and my mother, too, but he said, No, do not speak, you will wake the spirits of the field, and I laughed because I saw nothing but the growing corn swaying with a murmur, casting, when the moon was out (the moon, the soft, secret, sad moon), long pointed shadows and I would say, I see the spirits now, there, there and there, quickly, look, and then he would laugh, his arms strong about me, so sheltering that I never wanted to leave the field, and I wanted to be always a child so that the day would go away like the clouds that disappeared when I lay on the ground staring at the sky, that it would disappear and melt into the night, when again we would lie in the field, and I would close my eyes and forget the silent woman who hated me although I did not know why, whom I must never touch because she would scream, evil, why do you torment me? . . . you, his child, his the evil, and then she would weep and say, god, god, god, who I knew was in the sky, who the people in the village said was holy and good and just but whom the man my father hated when he dug into the earth for the roots to clear the land where later he would plant corn, which grew very long during the season when he would guard the crop and I would grow with him, those days when the moon came out very round, very bright, very sad, and, Why does she not come out in the day? I asked, and my father said, The moon is a sad lonely woman, very sad and lonely, and I said, Why? . . . and if she is sad, why does she not shine in the day with the sun? . . . And I was staring into the night where no sound came except the occasional hooting of an owl. And he held me in his arms because suddenly I was afraid of the sadness of the moon, afraid it would come down and make me itself also, so that I too would live only in the night.

And my father said, "In the morning of the world before there was day and the moon saw the sun waiting for the day and the moon thought he was beautiful and her heart burned with longing, and she thought, Surely whoever made me will place me next to my lover, and I will weave a marriage hammock until he comes to me, but time came and the sun was the day and the moon the night, and the moon wept with unbearable love, long-

ing still for the day when she would fuse with her lover, and so
she continues weaving the bridal hammock, and she clothes herself in pure-white veils, pure for the sun to take her in the ecstasy
of fulfilled desire, but time passes, and still the sun comes in the
day and the moon in the night, and the moon sighs, Come to
me, come to the hammock which I have woven, but she sinks
into the sea because the day has come, and so the veils grow
ragged, the marriage veils she wears when in her journey toward
morning she crosses the sea watching herself in the water hoping
for the time of consummation, and the hammock grows and
grows because the sun never comes, never hears the lonely sighing, never knows the sad aching, never feels the great love, and
so the moon still searches for her lover the sun. And see, there,
and over there, see?, he said pointing to the moon, there are its
worn marriage veils. And I looked into the sky, and there was the
moon, and about her the thin white clouds, and, Yes, I said, but
if it is very lonely, why does it not marry the stars? And my father
said, Because it does not love the stars, it loves the sun, and so its
soul (What is the soul? I asked, and he answered, It is the bodiless life), and so the moon's soul must search in loneliness forever
until time ends, and when he had finished speaking, I clung to
him because I was sad for the moon, who must hunt forever, and
soon the man who was my father was asleep, but I could not
sleep, because when I closed my eyes I imagined the moon had
stepped from the sky, that it stood, a white-veiled woman, before
me, weeping, and that those tears would cover me as she moved
toward me to embrace me with her sadness . . . until I screamed
and my father woke stroking my hair, until the sun came out
expelling the night, until, again, he had to face the silent woman,
my mother."

And so time passed, time in which I grew, time in which I
no longer questioned the silence of the woman, time in which I
went with my father into the field during the season of the grow-

ing corn, time in which I wandered through the village and the women turned from me and hid their children from me, time in which I went, when there was no one, to the small church, where the doll had been broken, and where once there was a man sitting in the darkness where there were no candles, and that man was dressed in black, and I had seen him come one day and all the women knelt at his feet kissing the hem of his robe, which was long, and all the children kissed his hand. He was a man who had come like the others, who didn't stay long, replaced by others, who left soon too, but this one would stay longer, and I was standing before the doll whose head was no longer broken and whose face was colored more brightly now, when that man in black came to me and he stood in the light of the candles, and he was old and his hair was white and his face smiled and there was a white collar about his neck and his voice was soft as he said, I have not seen you before, do you come here to pray? I did not answer because I did not understand, until the soft voice said again, Do you come to ask the virgin for help? Do you come to speak to the great god? And I understood, remembering what my father had said so often in the fields at night, and I said what he had told me, which was, The god is a stone face laughing in the night, and the brows of the man in black came together and the smile was still there but troubled and he placed his hand on my shoulder, as only my father had done, and I shuddered but did not turn away because his smile was gentle as the voice said, The god is kindness and not-anger, not-hate. I, still remembering the words of my father, said, The god is the angry stranger who separated the moon from her lover and set the souls of the dead to wander in the night as animals. And the man dressed in black with the clean white collar said, The god is . . . but he stopped, still smiling, and then he said, But you are very young, still a child, will you come back often? I turned from him, facing the tiny doll, and said, Yes, because his

face was kind and his voice was soft and his hand on me was
kind and soft, and I said, Yes, again, turning to leave because I
knew that soon the silent woman would walk kneeling toward
the place where the cross was, beating her breast, but before I
could go, that man in black with the soft kind gentle gray eyes
held my hand, and I felt something small and I heard him say,
Carry this amulet of the virgin with you always, and outside in
the white blaze of the afternoon, the amulet which had first felt
cold felt warm, and I opened my hand and saw on it the face of
a beautiful woman—who looked strangely like my mother—and I
held it in my fingers feeling the tiny face which gleamed in the
sun, like the eyes of the man in black . . . but not dazzling like
the beads of the necklace that my father would give me later,
much later when I was no longer a child.

And still the bird time swept past through the endless sky of
eternity, and I did not return to the man in black because always
there were people with him, but I kept the amulet with me never
showing it to my father until one day walking to the field
(although I was no longer a child, I went with him still to the
milpa) through the village where the women turned from us, and
I could hear their frightened whispering and could not understand, then walking through the brush and the trees, hearing
the rustle of the animals, holding the hand of my father, I said,
It is an owl, and he said to himself, because he did not look at
me, No, it is the spirit of one dead and not yet at rest, and I held
his hand tighter, and he went on still to himself, The lonely long
for death, but death is not peaceful, and there are those that say
that the dead do not return to this world, because who will long
for the dark where there is infinite light? And who will search
for the desert where the sky is inverted into a pool of water? . . .
but those who believe and have never seen the laughing stone

face of god (I was holding the amulet secretly in the hand which he held as we walked through the brush), they do not know that the unresting souls of sad wanderers return to this former world even in death, still to be punished for life, and these are the spirits that possess the bodies of the jungle animals, these the spirits doomed to wander in death as they wandered in life, these the spirits that search the warmth of life in other bodies, lonesomely wailing, tortured, those sad wanderers, and the snake possessed must never cross the path of a man because that will be death in life, and if it touches his feet, that man will know sorrow forever and so his family too, and their family forever until the end of time—unfairly—and we had come then to the cross that marks one of the four entrances to our village, and the bones of an animal lay there and over the bones from the branches of a tree hung a small very faded doll, and the man shuddered, and he turned from it, and he said he did not know what the doll and the bones meant, but he said that the woman who had raised him as a son had told him that once in the long, long past a boy and a girl had loved beneath the shadow of that cross and they were discovered and sent from the village, while the people flung stones at them, first at the girl as the boy watched, then at the boy, driving them in opposite directions, so they would be lost in the jungle and never together. And now my father was holding my hand very tightly and he held my fingers and then he felt the amulet in my hand and he asked where it had come from, and I told him of the man and I told him of that man's god which was not-hatred, not-anger, kindness, and the man turned from me and stood very straight looking into the sky, and I said, What are you searching? He faced me furiously, shouting, Give it to me, and he tore the amulet from my hands and flung it far into the greenness where I could not find it, where I searched and searched—and he helped me, too, now kind—searching for the lost amulet, and he said without anger, I will get you a necklace prettier and brighter, and it will make you very, very happy—so that I never went back to the man in black, so that I thought always of the amulet and of the secret woman on it.

One day a man came from the modern city of the Mexican people of the flourishing race and the children of the village ran to him, joining hands forming a circle about him, and they sang and he laughed, and the mothers came and gathered about him, and he was not dark and his hair was very brilliant, and he opened his mouth and half of his teeth were gold, and the women sighed and the children shouted happily (and I was in the distance and they had not seen me) because this was the holy-day excitement of the men who came from the city period-ically, selling dazzling jewels and beautiful-colored cloths, which the people bought sometimes but did not wear, which they fold-ed neatly and put in boxes, which they showed to their neigh-bors but did not wear, which they gave to the wives of their sons before their marriages, who did not wear them but put them in boxes, showing them to their neighbors but never, never wear-ing them, and the man smiled opening his mouth showing the dazzling golden teeth, and he sat there in the middle of the ground, and he was very happy and his hands worked quickly moving like the flames of fire, doing this as he showed the bright earrings and bracelets, putting them into his mouth showing again the jeweled teeth and biting the beads to show the people the enormous value of the stones, holding them up to the sun, so that those people with the gaping mouths could see how pure was the work that the stone did not stop the light from passing through, sitting there with the women and the young girls and the children hovering over him all afternoon, until the sun sank into the distant *milpas*, from which the men would be returning, and the women returned to their thatched

houses with the children and the dogs following happily, leaving
the man of the golden mouth sitting there counting the coins
which the women had given him, sitting there folding the cloths
which were not sold, carelessly tossing the precious stones of
many colors which he had tested by biting and holding against
the sun, which had almost faded, so that the man looked about
him noticing the coming darkness, looked about and saw me,
and he smiled but not like the man in black to whom I did not
return who had given me the amulet which was lost, buried in
the soil, in the past, and standing grinning at me, his teeth were
no longer golden because the light did not shine on them and
they were dull and those that were not yellow were brown and
dirty and he stood before me, and he said, You did not see the
necklaces, here, and he brought one before me, and he was saying, These are the most valuable, they cost very, very much in
the city from which I come, and he said, You must have one,
and he was still looking at me, and then he said, You are more
beautiful than the necklace but the necklace will make you even
more beautiful, do you want this necklace? and I said, I do not
want it, because the man was frightening and ugly in the coming
night, and he said, I will give it to you anyway if you will let me
touch you, and then he was looking about him, and everything
was dark now and it was night, and when he was searching he
saw a man coming toward us and his face changed quickly and
his smile faded and he began fingering the necklaces in the box
busily, and the man he had seen was my father returning from
the *milpa*, and my father stared darkly at the man of the dull
teeth and said to him, You have necklaces to sell? The yellow-
toothed man said yes, smiling again as with the women previously, and my father took the necklaces and he looked at each one
carefully and there was one that he liked, and the man of the no-
longer-gleaming teeth said, Yes, that is the prettiest, it is the most
valuable one too, one which I did not show the other women

because they cannot wear it, but this girl here she may wear it as proudly as the grand women of the city from which I come, see, and he held it up, and my father took it and put it about my neck and he took my hand and we walked to the house and returned to the man and gave him the coins he had asked for, and my father said to him, Go now quickly and never come back here to the girl.

At night lying in the hammock I looked at the necklace and remembered the amulet whose place the necklace was taking, and wanted the amulet of the woman's face which the man in black had given me, and I took the necklace that night and placed it in a small box and left it there, until . . .

But this I will not tell you, this must remain in the secrecy of memory. And yet that memory comes upon me covering me like the sea, like time, like the waves sweeping over the shore which cannot resist this, this . . .

And then the boy came.

And my life changed.

And my soul opened to receive him.

And I loved him with the intensity of my soul and heart and body, and with aching even greater because it was the longing of unrealized love, I felt the loneliness in him and did not understand, and longed vainly, and I felt the strangeness and the mystery and the desperation and the animal franticness . . . and did not understand.

And then he was gone.

And still I loved him.

And my soul that had opened to him closed like the flowers that close to the moon.

I left the village of the silent woman and of my father whom I knew I must leave now forever, and I ran and walked in the furiously blazing sun, ran—somewhere—to the modern city of the flourishing race of the Mexican people, to find the boy whom I love, feeling the scorched earth burning my feet, the heat like a stone upon my back, and the thirst, and the pain of unrealized desire, walking and running through the angry green land until I realized I was lost, until I could see nothing but the whirling light of the sun, until the clouds came with the rain and I fell to the ground.

And yet I know I will find the city, and I will find the boy, and then he will take me, my body and my soul.

4

On the hammock the girl stirred. She opened her eyes, and she was awake now, and conscious. Her eyes searched the room. She saw the old man, and she saw the old woman and the fading skeleton sleeping in the corner of the small room.

Then she looked through the window, where it was night. The rain drummed on the thatched roof.

The clouds parted, and the moon shone momentarily like a frantic woman.

The girl in the hammock seemed to be drowning in the white light.

THREE: The Man

I

In the village from which the girl had come her father sat thinking without knowing his thoughts. He sat on the moist ground. The woman knelt before the *metate*, kneading with slow rhythmic movements the maize for the tortillas.

It was still raining, and the world was smothered by the haze of the gray sky. The verdure was dark green. And the man knew that when the rain stopped, he would have to fell the brush again. The trunks would sprout, roots buried. The land would be mud.

Then the field became unimportant in the man's mind.

Looking at the hammock by the window, he thought, *She will never return, that girl.* Then he thought, *What is left? The woman*, he thought. He thought, *My wife. Passion?* he thought. He remembered the day before, the woman lying dead-like beneath him, himself trying to destroy the angry negating god within her, trying to fire what had been smothered so long ago.

Lust, he thought.

And then involuntarily his mind evoked the boy of the lithe body and the desperate eyes.

He put his hands to his head to stop the storm of memory. But his thoughts persisted. *Now the girl is gone to search for him, and now I am alone.*

The rhythmic movements of the woman continued steadily.

Then the man saw a scorpion the size of his hand. It writhed on the dirt, its tail raised waiting. The man stared fascinated. The beautiful, hideous thing did not feel.

Gratification, the man thought.

He thought, *It does not feel. It hunts.*

Now the scorpion moved swiftly leaving a trail on the moist earth. Then it stopped before something green.

The man rose. He saw the green something come alive, move. It was an insect, the kind that blends into the green of this country and comes with the rain, and it moved again. And the man, standing very close, saw that it had terrible unseeing eyes.

And the man saw himself on the same damp earth, saw himself as the scorpion. *The hunter who does feel, who lives. Gratification*, he thought. *It does not feel.*

The scorpion reached out with pincers for the animate leaf of the unseeing eyes. The man saw those eyes grow hideously and burst. He saw himself sting the green thing, killing the eyes. But the eyes, bursting, had come alive instead, and they were gazing and depthless, abysmal.

The scorpion drained the struggling leaf and slowly the insect shrank like a desiccated old woman, shriveling. And the scorpion drained that other life into itself, becoming more powerful, having two lives. Nothing remained of the insect but a tiny shell. The scorpion stood triumphantly.

Then the man raised his bare foot over the scorpion. (I who have two lives . . .) He mashed the thing with his naked foot. The thing squirmed once, and the man brought his foot over it again and again until nothing was left but liquid next to the empty shell of the insect.

And the man felt strong and powerful, liberated by the scent of death. Feeling a surge of strength, he turned triumphantly to the woman.

But her eyes were firmed intently on the mixture of maize before her.

Looking at her, he felt powerless again, and desperately alone.

He sat wearily on the ground.

And memory, unleashed by the struggle of the scorpion and the insect and himself, carried him like a powerful wind.

2

I the man.

I too am silent.

If I could speak, if I could stand futureless on the moment of present and gaze into the vastness of the past, if I could let the waves roar over the shore of present, unmolding in a moment what was molded before birth, if I could shape the pain, the longing, the loneliness, the long-sought love, if I could bring forth the reasons clutched in my hands, the long-buried secrets for which the tongue cannot form words.

If I could speak.

That in memory and even beyond memory, there is this . . .

The moon cast gray shadows and the air was still. The only sound was that of the leaves as a man made his way through the jungle. He stumbled, and he looked about in terror, clutching the holy amulet about his neck. He rose again and ran into the night.

Among the trees, embraced by them, was the house of the old woman.

"Old woman," he called softly.

A feeble voice summoned him in.

The woman he sought was before him.

And the gray light of the moon fell on one side of her face only, the other side drowned in the thick dark of night.

"I have come for help, old woman," said the man.

The wrinkled lids of the old woman's eyes opened, but although the moon illumined a whole side of her face, the eye there was lusterless and dead.

"Old woman, in the village a child is dying. I am his father."

"You are the father of the dying child," the old woman echoed, and her voice, ancient and feeble, nevertheless filled the room.

The father sat on the dirt before this woman who knew the secrets of life.

"The h-menob," she said, "those holy men have seen the child?"

The man nodded.

"And they can do nothing?"

"They cannot cure him," said the father. "He has been bled. But my son is still dying."

"They do not know of the soul," the old woman said, the line of her mouth converging contemptuously with the wrinkles about her nose and chin.

"But you who are ancient, who know life, you can help me," said the man.

The ancient woman stood silhouetted against the moon. The features of her face were smothered by the dark. Only the outline was luminous. It was as if she were burning in cold-white fire.

The man of the dying child reached for the rotting dress to kiss it. But the woman moved away fiercely.

"No," she shouted. "Would you dare to touch god?"

The white stringy hair on her head was like a mat of cobwebs, and it seemed to the man that if a breeze entered the room, the hair would be blown awry and spiders would rush from the head.

"I will help you," said the old, old voice. Then it rose and was almost young as she said, "I have known of the child, and of the sickness, of the birth . . . for such things are known to me."

"How can I save his life?"

A thin veil of a cloud obscured the moon. The woman waited until its light shone again. With the return of light, she seemed to see the man for the first time.

"Blood," she shrieked, crouching on the ground.

The man recoiled. He wiped off the blood. "As I ran to you, I fell."

"Yes," the woman hissed.

The cobwebbed hair trembled, and the man watched terrified for the spiders that would surely come, but the woman no longer moved, and the hair was still, and the man breathed more easily as the woman hissed, "Yes, and I know over what you fell." Her shoulders, thin and decrepit, were like the wings of a new-born bird.

The man felt fear, sharply. He wanted all motion to stop, all sound, so that the cobwebbed hair would not move, not shake forth the spiders which his mind imagined.

"It was the head of the Pol,"[11] the old voice said deliberately.

"No," the man said, and he looked out the door into the black waiting jungle, wanting to flee from the horror, to leave behind the fear piercing him like a cold knife, to return to the side of his dying child, where the holy men chanted to keep him alive, away from this old, ancient woman, away from the cobwebbed hair.

The white-burning head was raised very proudly. "If you do not want to save your child, go . . . go quickly."

---

[11]Refers to an evil woman who practices sorcery.

"Tell me," said the man, "I will not doubt you again." He cast down his eyes, so that he would not see the hair. He reached for the rotting dress once again. But he stopped.

"Your wife," came the inevitable words of the woman.

"She is good," the man said. "She is always with the child. And she prays. She is not evil. She has always been faithful."

"Evil," said the old woman. "Evil can enter even the good and contaminate the heart. For it is powerful. And it plants itself in the greatest of hearts. It gnaws the heart and plants its seeds. And then comes its fruit." And she said, "With you your wife is always silent now. And her eyes gaze upward, listening to other voices."

The man remembered. He saw his wife kneeling beside the hammock on which the child had lain for seven days. He saw her gazing toward heaven—in *supplication*, he thought. *But that, that was praying. And yet . . .*

"Yes, it is so," he said.

The wrinkles of the old woman loosened into the vestige of a smile. "The Pol," she said, her voice reverberating in the darkness. Then her voice rose full and almost young, and although the man knew the ancient story of evil like the others of his people, the woman chanted the legend, and her spider-hands dug into the earth, holding the dirt in her palms.

The voice told the story of the wife who had been beyond the understanding of her husband, so that although he begged her to speak, she remained impassive, separated from his world as if attuned to something vastly mysterious.

As the chanting voice of the old woman continued her ancient tale, the father of the dying child stared at the moon through the window, and the moon sighed sadly as if this ancient old woman was spinning her tragedy.

But the husband of the woman, the chanting voice continued, had not been of those who can delve into the soul, not of those who can dissect the heart and let the blood flow black. And so he saw only physical evil, and he thought his wife was unfaithful, and so he had been stung by the serpent of jealousy, which many say is deadlier than the serpent Uolpoch.

For many days the man did not go to his *milpa*, to keep his wife from the lover he imagined, but one morning he rose saying that he would stay in the field guarding the corn, but he thought, I will return early, I will discover her lover. And so he walked a great distance into the jungle to give the woman time to meet her lover, and as he walked, the animals possessed by the spirits of the dead warned him, *Do not return to your house, stay in the field.*

But the man of the mysterious wife was deafened by jealousy and he returned to the house. And when he entered, he saw lying on the *metate* where the maize is ground for the tortillas the head of his wife. The head was alive, for the eyes rolled in supplication, but no words came. In terror, the man fled to the oldest and holiest of the holy men of his village, who explained that the woman was a sorceress who, at will, when the sun fell, could transform her body into an animal. But only her head must remain behind, while the body searched through the jungle bringing evil.

How can I destroy this evil? How can I free myself?

There is a way.

Tell me. I will know. I have seen evil.

I will tell you. But if you speak what I will say, the eagle will split your skull, the serpent will sting your breast, the dark rock will open its womb to you, and you will drown forever in blood.

And so before the rising of the sun, the husband of the sorceress returned to his house. He ground the salt quickly for the charm, as the holy man had instructed, and he made the necessary movements and muttered the magic words.

Groans rose from the tortured lips of the woman's head.

Wipe off the salt, pled the head, for her husband had touched the neck with the magic salt. Why do you do this? I have always loved you, but evil spirits possess me and I must wander in the night. Yet I have loved you always, and I have waited until you were gone, that you would not feel the evil. Oh, wipe off the salt.

But the man felt the strength of love and he would save the sorceress, but the sun came out and the groaning stopped, and the mouth was shut. And the man ran into the jungle and did not return.

"The head still searches for the body, even as the Xtabay searches for love," the voice of the ancient woman rose, "and the evil spirit assumes other forms and brings evil. And through the trees the lonely wailing is heard, the mourning of the evil Pol, who must wander forever, even in death, forever until time ends, searching for what she will never find. For there is no substitute for salvation. Her evil is powerful, for it is the evil of isolation. And that evil is alive. Your wife . . . Evil can enter the good and contaminate the heart. . . . "

The man sat resignedly, knowing the implication of the woman's words. He saw the leaves of the trees rustled by a slight breeze, and he wanted to stop the breeze before it entered, rousing the spider-webbed hair of the old woman. But the breeze died outside.

"These many days I have known of you and your child," the old woman said. "And I have sat in the night watching the moon, waiting for you to come. Voices have spoken and said, the Pol possesses this man's wife, and his child's innocence is fed by the juice of evil, but youth is of good, and so the child is dying. The more he resists, the more he nears death, for death purifies, and the child longs for purification."

The moon receded in terror behind the clouds. And silence burst loudly in the room.

The old woman advanced toward the man. She knelt before him, and her hair almost touched him.

He recoiled, staring at the luminous-white hair, at the horrible network of cobwebs.

Closer, the old woman moved. She raised one slowly rotting hand to her mouth. "Your wife is . . . evil."

She stood rigid, thin and cadaverous, arms stretched to the moon, and her neck strained like the dried twig of a once-great tree.

Through the thatch of the house, a gust of wind entered passing through her hair. The hair trembled, and the man watched in horror. *The spiders,* he thought wildly, clutching for the ground, to rise, to run. *The spiders, the spiders.*

But when the air was calm again, unmoving, the cobwebs were intact.

The mother of the dying child knelt before the hammock in the moon-bathed room. Where the thatch was thick, the light did not enter, and the darkness swirled in thick black pools. The eyes of the woman were closed, as if to squeeze from her body some pain.

In the hammock the dying child lay, quiet, tiny, his mouth open.

The mother muttered something, tightening her clasped hands.

Once the child squirmed, and she made a motion to touch him. But a hand was laid heavily on her shoulder, stopping her.

It was the hand of the holy man, who stood drunkenly behind her—a dark-brown hand, with long fingernails that had begun to curve inward like the claws of an old dog.

The man was very ugly. His hair was white and long, as if allowed to grow to subdue the hideous appearance, the toothless mouth, the vicious eyes. His father had been a holy man, and that father's father before him.

Standing over the kneeling woman, his back to the anxious group of men and women lining the wall watching the holy ritual, he felt powerful. In his left hand he held a dead chicken, which he raised the length of his arm, over the hammock, the fowl hanging grotesquely over the child. He twisted the neck of the chicken as if to squeeze from it even the vestige of life.

The mother's face was set, as if molded of hardened clay. Without looking up, she knew what the holy man was doing. She stared harder at the child as the holy man squeezed the neck of the chicken even tighter. And she expected life to flow into the fading child as it flowed from the chicken. But the child remained the same, and the holy man squeezed the neck of the animal.

Another woman entered the room. She was large and she panted audibly. Religiously, devoutly, she carried the plants she had been sent out to gather, the *zipche*, the roots of *xul*. These she laid reverently on a table. She made the sign of the cross, reaching for someone's hand in order to kneel.

Now the holy man released the chicken. It fell at the feet of the mother, who picked it up and carried it quickly to the table, returning to kneel by the hammock again.

About the chicken, about the plants, two women worked urgently, the fat woman recited the magic words.

The holy man grumbled instructions to the women, his filthy hand reaching for the bottle of rum which he would soon offer to the winds.

Sighing, he walked into the night. The sight of the freezing moon made him shudder, and he drank from the bottle, surrendering to the drunken stupor he had almost been in since earlier that night when he had been summoned to the side of the dying child. And the holy man closed his eyes and slept.

The moon watched. Misty veils concealed the weeping face. The sky was frozen.

Inside, women clustered over the dead chicken. Soon it would be midnight. The fat woman was chanting the Catholic prayers now, having exhausted those of the ancient religion.

"*Creo en Dios padre, Todopoderoso . . .*"[12]

The mother of the dying child seemed unaware of all about her, as if she was in a trance where only she and the child and something intangible and evil existed. Occasionally she grasped her long tense neck as if to choke a cry of terror or pain.

"*Creo en el Espíritu Santo . . .*"[13]

At midnight, one of the women roused the holy man, touching his shoulder because she dared not shake him. She was immediately aware of the moon.

"It is Friday now," she whispered. "It is midnight."

The holy man rose laboriously. He entered the room, and the vicissitude of men and women, of thatch and *metate*, of hammock trembled before him. He reached for the arm of the woman beside him. In his left hand he still held the bottle of rum. The room settled before him, and he was able to move slowly.

On the table was the prepared offering, the boiled fowl, and, under all this on the ground, the dish of claws, beak, feathers, the viscera of the strangled chicken.

The holy man, still moving uncertainly toward the hammock, began to chant, partly to regain his consciousness. Then his mind cleared miraculously, and he was summoning the spirits, making the offering to the winds, mourning the dying child.

---

[12] I believe in God all powerful.
[13] I believe in the Holy Spirit.

"Cu yantal u xolcab ti kubah ahkin idzac, u likez u tzel uay tu tan mesa huntal chaac . . . . "

"I kneel to offer this which is now before the table of the chaac . . . . "

Then the father of the dying child entered the room.

No one noticed him.

All were caught in religious rapture. The mother's face was ecstatic in her world of self, child and intangible unseen evil, mouth open, eyes closed, hands clasped, as if something glorious would descend upon her. The fat woman rocked to the h-man's chanting, moaning silently in religious passion, feeling all at once the awe of fearing the mysterious god, the secret spirits. Even the men in the room had knelt, carried by the tide of ecstasy, seized, rocked, swept, consumed, entranced, and the feeling of affinity to god in each of them, through suffering, reached its zenith, and there was perfect silence, very, very suddenly, but the motions continued in pantomime, each listening to his own inner music.

The father of the dying child saw his wife against the moon-pierced thatch, her neck arched. He saw his child, saw the holy man performing the ceremony, saw the people kneeling. And then he saw the bottle of rum, the offering under the table.

He reached for the bottle. With a crashing sound the bottle shattered over the offering. The rum poured over the feathers, beak, claws. The spell was broken. The father shouted angrily to the men and women. His hands lifted the table that the women had prepared, and the offering spilled on the ground, over the rum.

"Go," he shouted.

The holy man reached for the hammock, the room reeling, colors blending into colors, into one terrible burst of white. He moved against the thatched wall, groping. Something exploded in his mind, the room became a dreadful sea of mouths gaping in horror ready to swallow. The moon rushed through the thatch, shattering his face, embracing him with cold fingers. Darkness sprang from the floor and lifted a shroud over him. He sank to the floor.

The father of the dying child ran through the room, pushing at the people, past them, between them. "Go."

The mother rose from the ground, the world of self-bursting. Her hands grasped her neck, the fingers tightening about it as the holy man's fingers had tightened about the strangled chicken.

"I do not need you," the father shouted at the people. "The child does not need you, go, you cannot help him."

Voice blended into voice, into the noise of stamping feet. The previous silence had accumulated sound as a cloud collects rain, and now it showered over the room like stones dropped into stagnant water setting everything into motion.

"He is mad," screamed a woman.

The man, looking at the retreating shadows pushing against the door, saw instead the veiled moon.

He turned from it. He rushed toward the child and grabbed it from the hammock, clutching it as he stared with hatred at his wife. Now husband and wife stood in the darkness where the light from the moon could not enter, but each was completely aware of the other. In the man's arms, the child began to cry. The mother now moved about the room like a caged animal, toward the door as if to summon the people back, then approached her husband with hands reaching for the child.

Neck stretched in supplication, she threw herself at his feet.

He moved away. The woman fell to the ground. Her hand fell on something sharp, and she was aware of something piercing her neck. She tore at her throat and saw the claws of the strangled chicken.

The husband saw her bleeding neck, and in his mind he saw the pounding veins. *The source of evil*, he thought. *The coursing blood feeding this child.*

Your wife . . . is . . . evil. . . .

In his mind, a river rushed flooding the village. Then the river was a sea, and the man heard the roaring. The river, the sea. Ocean . . . . Waves beat against the shore of his mind, the village sank, the water rose reaching for the moon. The tide receded, and he saw, silhouetted, the neck of his wife stretched pleading.

Your wife . . . is . . . evil. . . .

He stood over her, petrified momentarily with fear, fear of the old woman in the jungle, fear of his wife, fear of the sad moon—the fear of one who knows he is facing evil.

"I know," he whispered to the woman.

"My child," the woman wept. "Give me my child."

He held his son almost smothering him.

"To feed him your evil juice, to make him an evil wanderer like yourself, to contaminate him?"

"My child," wept the woman.

The man shook his head, for the fantastic moon, stripping herself of the thin veils of clouds, sprang into the house illuminating the woman's head, but the rest of the woman, the prostrate body, wallowed in the quicksand of darkness.

The lips moved, but no sound came.

The man moved to where the table had fallen, where the knife which the women had used to prepare the chicken for the purification lay. He thought, *The salt, now only the salt for the true purification.*

The knife was cold in his hand, and it was as if he held a piece of the moon.

"Why?" pled the urgent voice of the mother, seeing the knife. "I have always been faithful to you, always loved you."

But evil spirits have possessed me and I must wander in the night.
"Tell me what I have done."
I have waited until you were gone, that you would be spared the evil.

The husband no longer heard his wife's voice, but he saw the light-suspended head and heard, as if from another world, the reverberating echo.

The head still searches for the body.

The knife in his hand, ready, the child in the curve of one arm, he stood over the woman. But before he could execute the purification, he uttered a gasp of horror, a cry like the wail of a dying dog, and he plunged himself outside with the child tight in his arms.

The woman cried after him, shrieking.

Outside, the man was already disappearing, running through the thickness of the weeping trees, through the clouds of dark that swirled like silent wind, running through the gasping heat, piercing the thickness of the trees, the dark, the heat, piercing them with the cold knife, running into the waiting embrace of the shattered wailing moon.

The moon. . . .

3

I, the man.
What would I tell?
This.

Of that night running in the arms of my father, of the heat and the dark trees, of the pain, of the cold knife pressed against my flesh, of the night caving in like black stones, of the beginning of anger and hatred of loneliness and isolation, of destruction, and of the beginning of the search.

And we moved from place to place.

There was a small village, like the one we had left and those we would come to, which was very small, and it was of those same people of my race who had fled from the modern world of the Mexican people, of those same people who lived in thatched houses like small hills of grass, built about the *cenote*,[14] where the water was, where trees hung shelteringly over the small man-made hills of grass, where there were the mounds of white stones marking the place of someone dead next to the living who lived inside the small houses of thatch letting few people enter their village except those who bought the *chicle*,[15] from which they lived and from their *milpas* in the season of the corn, and the people in that village were suspicious of a man with a child who was sick, and they said, He is fleeing someone, perhaps the great modern people, and they were very afraid, and they said, He is dangerous, so that we left that village and wandered through the wilderness, farther and farther away from the woman who was my mother, who remained behind forever, farther into the trees for a long, long time, until I myself could walk, because I was no longer sick and because I was growing,

We walked endlessly through the plants that tore my legs, reaching different villages even where they raised the *henequén*,[16] where my father labored, and still I was growing, and then we moved on, and there were the stone monuments, much later, before which he knelt reciting strange words, monuments with steps, with figures of men in feathers, figures of the sun (to whom, my father told me, had once been offered young warriors, upon those altars as the mighty rulers watched), strange in the

---

[14]A natural well or sinkhole in Yucatán and parts of Central America formed by collapsed limestone that exposes ground water. It was sometimes used by ancient Mayans for sacrificial offerings.

[15]Gum.

[16]A variety of an agave succulent.

wilderness of the jungle, with plants rising up the stones, and he told me also that these were infinitely old, and that they were of my race, of the ancient ones who had come long before me, and sitting under the sun that was like arrows piercing my back, he spoke of a very old people who were very, very great, and these people had flowered mightily like some luscious plant, and the god loved them but there came a time when a new people rose and the civilization of my people faded and the people separated and became wanderers (because, he said, the god had turned against those ancient people), and many, many years later, much later, many lives and deaths after, the race of the Mexican became powerful and there was fighting and blood and terror, and the greatness of my ancient race was gone, with one thing left which will remain forever, which are those monuments before which I stood, and so those my people had scattered into the hidden villages away from the cities and the flourishing race, and as my father spoke, I was thinking, *then this is the face of god, and there are the teeth and the eyes always watching,* of this god he spoke, yes, the god, who moves men as he wants, he said, who rules, who judges. And as he said this, his face was harsh and angry and he rose frighteningly, savagely, with a stone in his hand, and I cringed away from him in fear, wanting to run because I thought he would kill me, but he threw the stone angrily at the monument, the face of the powerful god. And then it was night and all was silent, and then I began to cry, afraid and hungry, longing for the woman whom we had left behind I knew now forever, and later we ate the deer that he killed and I felt better and by then I had forgotten the woman, perhaps completely and later forever, as I lay on the ground looking at the stars and the moon, who he said was searching for the sun, weaving a marriage hammock lonesomely which she would never use because the god who could do all—who created not only the earth and the sky but pain also—would never let the day and night fuse in ecstasy, and I looked at the stars, calm, yes, but only those stars, for my father was no longer lying beside me, and I called to him, and I shouted for him, and I was afraid of the dark, wondering where I would go if he had left me, and I remembered the villages where he had found water, and I was looking all around for him, and didn't see him but saw, instead, in the distance, the ghostly monuments now blue in the light of the moon—and they seemed to beckon me, and I imagined I heard my father calling me from that distant monument, where we had stood, he telling me of the ancient ones who had sacrificed the young to the angry god, and I was running like on that distant night, only now I was alone and I was no longer a child and there was no one to hold me, and my eyes widened with fear as I listened to the sound—that sound that I will always remember—and I ran toward the monument of the god that he had told me was of my people before me, and that monument moved farther until I shouted, Stop, still hearing the cry that called me, and magically the monument did stop, loomed before me with its huge evil face, so horribly that I did not dare come closer, and I thought, *I will run away forever,* but I heard a groan of pain again and the fear was gone at the gaping mouth of the god and I moved to the side where the sound came, where I saw my father lying against the stones of the monument that was god, and I saw what I thought was a red snake rushing out of his mouth, but when I stood before him, I saw it was blood, his blood, and the world rushed before me as I cried and clung to that man as he had held me that night long ago, trying to pull the knife which protruded from his chest, below his heart, doing this as he whispered coughing, My throat, yes, the evil woman possessed, hers, because I tried to take you from evil, and brought you more—the isolation—that same evil of the woman who bore you pursuing us, justly, because I failed to do what I must (and although I do not remember this, I will tell you what it was), destroy the source, her throat, my evil, evil, now the purification, rubbing the salt there, and then he coughed once more saying, The salt, the salt, and his head fell back at the same time that I pulled the knife from below his heart, and the snake flowed red, and looking up through the tears I saw the huge monument like a laughing face, and I heard the now-forever-silenced voice telling of the god of the ancient world who had forsaken his people, and a panther roared in my mind and body, biting, even in my hands, where the knife was dripping the thick black blood, and the monument laughed, god laughed, the evil, evil, evil god, and I flung the knife against the laughing face as I ran against the hard hated stone, beating it with my hands, kicking it, shouting at it, crying, reaching now for the knife to kill it.

And then I wandered alone.

I learned of the jungle and how to find water, for although the rain falls in torrents the earth rejects it in many places and the water flows from the surface and buries itself, and the yellow sun rose and became white and then orange and then again yellow and still I wandered, as I had with my father, only alone now, killing deer as he had shown me, and very often I would return to those monuments of the ancient dead and sometimes I would kneel as he had done, but later I came only to hate, standing, gazing at the face of the god, hating impotently because I could not hurt it, him, because it was great and I was small, because he would hurt me, as he had hurt my father and the people of my father before him, and sitting there, when the hatred was almost spent, I would watch the sun sink out of sight, just as the moon began its ascent, watching this, thinking I could hear it because again it had come too late for her lover the sun, so that it must continue forever to weave its hammock, but I thought, *Perhaps some day she will find the sun, and half the sky will be night and half will be day, and the moon will no longer weep and the search will have ended.* And thinking so, I fell asleep, sleep-

ing it seemed sometimes for long periods of time, which moved
meaninglessly, and then I reached that village where I was to
remain with a woman and a man who needed a son, remain
among those people who lived in the small houses about the
larger one where on top was the cross, where, the woman who
had taken me as son said, lived the god to whom I must pray in
order to live the good life, which she said is the un-sin and the
serenity of negation, but I would not go to that house of the
cross because they were wrong, because I knew where the real
god was, there in the black stone face of the monument, and he
was not the goodness and the not-loneliness but the cruel god
who had deserted the ancient race as he had deserted my father,
and so I was a stranger even to the woman and her husband,
and they brought men to see me, some who were of the village,
and made me stand in the field throwing the precious corn into
the wind and some wore white collars and were dressed in black
and they put drops of water on my head and they all asked me
of my people and withdrew from me when I answered that I was
of the ones of long ago who had sacrificed their warriors to the
sun, who had built the huge stone monuments on which was
the face of the god, who was powerful and cruel and would
never die, would live even after I had killed it with the knife
dropping blood snakes, and I told them I was one of those sacrificed, who had fought back, and then they left me for a long
time, until the season of the planting came, when I went to the
milpa with the man who had taken me as a son, where we slept
guarding the precious land, as he told me of the spirits who
haunt the fields, explaining the small altar in the *milpa*, and why
the ground must be blessed, why the *milpero* must never fell
more trees than necessary, why he must make offerings to the
chaacs and *balams*, the spirits of the field, why he must live the
good life, and he told me too of the evil that wanders in the
night, of the sad lost souls who did not find in death the peace

unfound in life, and, Why? I asked, and he answered, Because they were sinners and lived a life of turbulence, and so he spoke to those many lost souls who did not find even in death the peace unfound in life, who return seeking vainly the warmth of life, possessing the animals of the jungle, and once there was a snake in the field and the man shouted and held me tightly and the snake disappeared and the man knelt in prayer and told me this.

The snake is the bringer of evil who is possessed by one unresting, a soul destined to wander until time ends, and that snake must not cross the path of a man because if it touches his feet, that man will be doomed and his family after him and that family's family and those lives will be of sin and evil until at last will come the purification through complete negation, and I thought of those souls and of the unhappiness and the sadness and the loneliness, and I thought of those nights wandering in the jungle, and I felt again the consuming hatred for the god, but the man said the god was good and so he did not understand, and although he said this over and over lying on the ground looking at the inscrutable sky, and although he offered the maize to the spirits, and although he prayed to the god and his gods, and although once I knelt with him feeling peace, still the rains came early that season and the field was destroyed, and I knew it was that same stone face that had stared at me as I pulled the knife from my father's body long ago that had brought the rain, and I wanted to run back to that monument and ask and ask until I got an answer and then I would know and never wonder, never again wonder why in the next season the maize grew profusely, the same season when the man who had taken me as son died one night in his hammock, and I rushed to his side to pull out the knife, but this time there was no knife, no thick blood snakes, only the man dying, and when I raised my face to see the laughing gaping stone face, I saw only the sky through the thatch of the silent house, the rain-bringing sky that had destroyed the field long ago, and so this time the maize grew profusely and death came and I remained with the woman who spoke little now, that woman who had taken me as son, who sat gazing at the weeping sky now that her husband was gone, remained in the silent house, and so it was I went into the field daily, to rip the soil and defy those spirits of the pursuing god, and although I knew the futility of fighting, still I knew that I must fight, that although I could not stab god, as I had tried long ago, still I could struggle and not kneel as the others did, and my perspiration fell to the ground, and I thought, *This ground is mine, only mine, and my perspiration will run through its veins fingering my soil, and no holy man will step upon this earth, those* h-menob *of the ancient god, and the ground will be mine alone,* and the old woman who had taken me as son remained alone in that house, alone with me, until one day one of the very old ones of the village came and he spoke to that woman and she said only, Yes, not hearing what was said, looking out the window where her husband had gone, and the old man called me, looking at me, saying, Yes, it is time, and so, yes, it was time, because in the time that followed—time, to which sometimes I wanted to cling, for now I knew of death—the man whom they called the *casamentero*[17] would come late in the night for rum which the woman provided, and that matchmaker returned thus three times, and on the fourth time I must go with him, standing before the parents of the girl, silently hearing the *casamentero* praising my powers as a man (I who had not long discovered the mysteries of the body), and the old people nodded, but the girl was not there, and then finally I saw her, feeling more maleness than before, and I wanted her very much as we were led to the church where I had not entered until then, which now I must

---

[17]A matchmaker.

enter, because the new excitement was bursting in me for the girl beside me, and then it was finished and we walked to the house of the old woman, who still stared into the empty sky, the girl walking with me dressed in white, followed by those whom they called the *padrinos*,[18] then the four called the witnesses, and the girl extended her hand to the woman gazing through the window, I doing the same to those of her family, then sitting across from each other, hearing, *En el nombre del Padre, del Hijo, del Espíritu Santo*,[19] hearing also the *padrino* speaking of the holiness of marriage, hearing but only words, for I was looking at the girl whom I had married, so very young, so beautiful, so afraid, but I did not see her fear, only her, and I felt my body grow with longing and desire, and then I was with her, and she was still and silent, as I thought, *She too is mine, as the soil of my milpa is mine,* and I wanted my perspiration to run through her veins as it ran through the earth's, and I discovered her body, and for once I forgot the angry face of god, the knife, the thick red snakes of blood, and I thought only of the miracle of the flower opening to my touch as the remembered words of the marriage echoed in my mind,

. . . *yoklal beyo hach cimacol yacunticob—*

that they may be happy in the love of one another.

But the flower closed, and it was the face of the monumental god I had tried to kill.

And time that I could not cling to swept past in the rain-bringing sky.

Yet out of the closed flower the child came, growing in the dark shadows of the woman's hatred, the unbroken silence of

---

[18]Godparents.

[19]In the name of the Father, the Son, and the Holy Ghost.

the tight cruel lips which once I had pressed to my own—beautiful, this child, as if the once-beauty of the mother, now drowned in her vengeance, had planted its seed to grow more profusely into greater beauty because that seed must struggle for life against the smoldering waves of the mother's hatred.

Time, in which the moon rose weeping, carrying her sad empty hammock, and fell still searching. Time, in which the child who was mine grew into a girl, in which I found again the opened flower, and happiness somewhere away from the menacing stone face of the god, the face of the sky, the face of hatred that was my wife.

That girl, my daughter . . .

And then the boy came.

But I will not remember. Yet . . . that boy of the lithe body, the desperate eyes.

But she will never find him.

She will be lost like the souls that wander in the night, lost . . . like myself.

4

The man stood staring at the cloud-smothered haze of the sun, which had fully risen. The rain still fell steadily. He bent down to the place where the scorpion lay mashed.

He remained looking intently at it for a very long time.

FOUR: The Woman

I

The woman knelt over the *metate* kneading the mixture of maize for the *tortillas*.

Her hands were gaunt, and the veins were stark and angered as the fingers wove urgently into the soft mixture. This task she was performing had long become an automatic one performed every day now many times for years. And the rhythm, steady and cadenced and almost musical, of the kneading, rolling, pressing, was a sound not to be noticed. What the woman was noticing now was the equally steady sound of the rain. She was tense listening to that sound, because she knew that once it stopped, the ensuing silence would unleash accusations from the past.

As she strained listening, the long hands not stopping, still kneading, she saw her husband, a heavy shadow against the door and the grayish haze of the early-morning sun.

He is staring at the sky again, but he knows now he cannot kill it, cannot kill the rain, cannot smother the angry sky, she thought. For she had seen the man kill the scorpion, had seen the anger surge into the one motion of his stamping foot. And she had known what it was he was killing, so that when the scorpion lay mashed, she had closed her eyes and breathed the suspended breath.

The rain must never stop, she thought. *The silence must not come. Memory, bringing the angry waves of the past.*

And even as she thought that, she could see herself drowning in the tempestuous sea of past. *But the waves must retreat,* she thought, *slowly like the falling of rain, and the sea will be calm.*

Then the coiled snake braided at the nape of her neck would loosen, the braids unwinding their tight embrace. Slowly like many fingers the hair would open like a strange flower, and the water would separate the petals, and her face would lie beneath the water, and the hair would be alive as the body sank downward into the blue abyss, resting there on the peaceful sand forever, and eternity and the mysterious god would claim her at last embracing her so, secretly, silently, serenely, and the water would hum a lugubrious requiem to her forever.

But before peace came, she knew, the storm must come, and perhaps there would be only the storm, no peace, no embrace of eternity, serenely. *And so the rain must continue,* she thought.

Involuntarily, she stopped moving. She listened tensely for the ever-softening sound. She heard her husband's breathing, but not the rain.

Not the rain, she thought frantically.

And then she heard it, softly, softly, and her movements began again, with the breathing, pressing, rolling the cadenced rhythmical movements.

And she thought, *That man is lonely, he needs me now.*

She smiled inwardly, her hands beginning now to form the tortillas.

Now it is he.

She placed the mixture of maize, thin and round now, over the heated stones.

He would speak, but I will not answer. I am alone now, as he is alone, but I do not need him. And so he will wither without his daugh-

ter, that girl whom I gave him, will wither without her who is gone, and he will die like a sun-scorched flower denied water.

And I will let his soul die, and rot. And the girl's soul will rot and die too, of her who is gone forever now. And the ancient evil will be dead at last, at last the vindication, and I will be pure and the sin will have been washed away. And my soul will flower after the body dies.

After the body dies, she thought, and she stopped, listening for the rain which seemed to come only from memory. It will *soon stop*, she thought, frantically clinging to the faint, diminishing sound. *It will soon stop*, she told herself insistently, only to keep from thinking what she already knew, It has stopped already, now there will be the sea of memory, the accusing waves of the past.

All movement ceased, all sound. She raised her face angrily to nothing, staring hard, her body rigid as she listened for the sound which had fully stopped.

Dropping her hands to her sides, the body relaxing, spent and empty, flotsam-like, she thought deliberately, *It is no longer raining.*

2

I, the woman.

I, too, know reasons.

And I am silent also.

If I could speak, oh if I could tear the flesh and find the source, if I could cry, this is the reason, this is why, because the heart knows reasons, because the heart knows why.

If I could clutch the past, if I could capture and hold it and destroy time, if then. I could release that sweeping past, to say, See, there and there, it was all as inevitable as time, shaped before me long, long ago, if I could bring forth the heart, the longing, the loneliness, the long-

*smothering love, if I could bring forth the sin, O god of the ancient
world, O god of the flourishing race.*

If I could speak, what would I tell?

That in memory and even beyond memory there is this.

A snake writhed.

The poison boiled within the body, coiled about the trunk
of a tree like a choking vine.

In the near distance an agouti[20] heard the rustling. It buried
its hind toes into the dry earth and listened.

The snake unwound itself, and it stood in awe of the orange
sun, for its body swelled with yearning and the deadly poison
boiled ready to spill.

The agouti moved through the bushes. It too turned its gazing eyes toward the sun, and its ears listened for the noise.

A deer disappeared into the brush, and the snake thought,
*It is the season of heat when the deer act strangely and that deer will
run into the village and someone will kill it, and the warm life will flow
from it with the blood, warm, so warm.*

And thinking that, it felt cold, and it longed for the feel of
the warm deer-blood flowing over its own body. Then it became
aware of the agouti. *It too is warm. It too has life. It too is fed by the
warm blood.*

Then they met, the two searchers. And each recognized
immediately the wanderer in the other, each felt the loss, the
pain, the loss and pain of the bodiless searching soul, the loss of
the former life.

They stood in the light of the drowning sun.

The snake looked yearningly toward the horizon.

---

[20]A good sized rodent from Central America, the Caribbean and South
America that is known for its agility, thanks to its long legs and hoof-like
claws. They are also valued for their meat.

Soon it will be gone, said the snake, watching the sun. Soon there will be not even the sight of warmth. And I am cold, so cold.

And I, said the agouti, following the gaze of the snake toward the sun and the sight of warmth, I too am cold. I too long for the warmth of life. I have searched for very long, so long. Yet once in that former life there was fulfillment.

And the gaze of the agouti went beyond the horizon, beyond the leaden sky, into memory.

I, said the snake dolefully, I too found fulfillment in that former life . . . but that was my sin.

The former life, repeated the agouti. Do you still remember? Do you still yearn? Its eyes filled with longing, and for a moment the agouti forgot the coming of the dreadful night when even the sight of warmth would fade.

The snake coiled on the ground, trying to squeeze from both the body and the earth whatever heat was in each, whatever of the former life.

It was so long ago, the snake said. But yes, I remember. Is it possible to forget?

I too remember, and yearn, said the agouti, burrowing its toes into the earth as if to summon back the former life, as if that life lay buried in the earth. There were moments when the loneliness fled, when there seemed to be happiness. That once . . . but those moments, so short, so seldom . . . And now I yearn. For the warmth, for the feel of the blood coursing through my own body. How I long to recapture that moment when . . . I must not remember. For I was a young man then, and now I am a sad wanderer.

Again, there was a rustling sound. Two deer fled gracefully over the bushes, and then they met, and then they fused.

The agouti and the snake stared with longing eyes. Then each turned painfully from the sight of the deer.

A moment in the embrace of eternity, thought the snake.

Is there a god for the damned? said the agouti. Is there salvation beyond damnation? Oh, where did it flee, that life? And why? And what is sin?

There is no god, said the snake, but the god of evil. Who else would have set me to wander thus? Forever. And sin?

It is happiness in a world of sorrow.

Oh, infinity is such a long, long time to wander, said the agouti. Look. Do you see that cross in the distance marking the entrance to the village? That is the path to my village. And it is there where in the former life I lay with the girl beneath the shadow of the cross, and . . .

No, said the snake harshly, and it turned involuntarily from the agouti as if feeling a burning pain. No, do not speak. The sin cannot be undone.

That is true, said the agouti. But she was so beautiful and her body was like honey, and when I entered her, it was like eternity embracing us, it was as if . . .

No, said the snake, again harshly. The past is dead, the sin committed. Again it turned its head.

And the agouti peered with anxious eyes toward the distant cross, where the shadows of the trees converged darkly.

I will go there, said the agouti, and I will lean against that cross, as on that day, when she and I . . . And there will be, not the past recaptured, but the warmth of the past in memory, the warmth of that separate body that was mine momentarily long ago. I am so cold, so very, very cold.

The agouti hurtled toward the cross, and the snake followed. This is the cross, said the agouti, sighing.

And the snake thought, *Yes, this is the cross where we lay, you and I, in that other life when I was a girl, and your body entered mine and we were one in the embrace of eternity. And you remember, as I remember, that moment in eternity. And then the beginning of the lone-*

liness . . . *do you remember that too?* And the snake thought, *Do you remember the sadness, and the stones with which they drove us from the village? Do you remember that? And here we are again beneath the shadow of that same cross, both wandering souls, lost, still lonely, and where is the embrace of eternity? Where is my young body like honey? Where is your body that trembled as you entered mine beneath the shadow of this cross?*

Yes, this is the cross, said the agouti and flung itself against it with a cry of desperation, remembering. *Yes, it was here that my body fused with hers.*

And the snake, cold, remembering now only the warmth of the joined bodies, forgetting the embrace of eternity, feeling no longer the flow of life from one to the other, longing only for the physical warmth of the blood, desperately, only for the touch of life, not love, for the feel of another body to warm its own icy flesh, lashed at the agouti with a terrible hissing sound, coiling its body choking the former lover, squeezing tighter and tighter, as once long ago his legs had tightened about her body and his life's fluid had flowed into her.

Then it remained coiled, feeling the warmth momentarily, the stolen warmth which even then was disappearing, fading from the body. And then the body of the agouti was cold, frozen, and the soul had left the borrowed body to wander again searching.

And the snake unwound itself and fled, leaving the agouti in the converging shadows of the cross and the trees, fleeing the last rays of the accusing sun, writhing.

In the near distance it saw the man who stood gazing latently before him, across the land.

That man stood by the path of the cross watching the sun pour fire over the earth beyond, and he was thinking serenely of the corn growing in his *milpa*, of the stalks bending to the cautious breeze, feeling the wonder of life, the wonder of peace, feeling that life was not evil, realizing at that moment that his toil in the field was its own reward, for the corn there would be high, proud, majestic.

Suddenly, the snake crossed the man's bare feet, its body writhing to steal the warmth of human flesh.

The man stared at the desperate thing, already disappearing into the bushes beyond the cross. Then he touched his feet where the body had passed.

He covered his face, smothering a cry of fear.

I, the woman.
What would I tell?
This.

That man was my father, and the snake of evil had crossed his path, and that was the beginning.

Nightly we prayed, my mother, my father, the brothers and sisters, the aunts. . . . Nightly we prayed to the great god, dear blessed god in high heaven, have mercy on the man whose feet have been crossed by the evil snake. But the inscrutable god in his infinite goodness did not hear, and in the night my father could hear noises in his *milpa* and he burned the maize to the winds and made altars to guard his crop, and he chanted prayers to the spirits and remained there in the night, but the animals came when he fell asleep, and the crop was gone that season, and later there was the fire consuming the next crop, and the flames danced, and so the evil had come like a rain plague in the village, and, still the praying continued, and then the little child who was my sister died one night while beside her my father sat weeping, and so the evil over and over, the evil sweeping like a howling wind, until one day the holy man came, a tall man who knew secrets and charms, who cured those touched by evil, who cracked the eggs and spilled the spirits and drove away the magic charms, who came that night so long ago (almost drowned in memory, yes, but present still, because the present is the ashes of the burned past and the essence of the future blending), and told us that evil could be conquered only by good, which is the life of abstinence, which is prayer nightly and fasting, and the *novenas*[21] to the wooden cross, and devotion to the mysterious gods, and silence in the house, where happiness must be excluded, because the holy man said that man was a small thing and that my father had sinned feeling himself a part of the god on that day when the snake had touched his feet in warning, and we all sat huddled in the black cave of our house, the h-men standing in the corner (and I could not see him, but I could feel him, could feel the heavy breath, could smell that breath, so sweet), repeating that my father had lured the snake with thoughts which elevated him and destroyed his humility, so that the angry god had sent the snake to bring the evil of the animals into the *milpa* and the fire burning the crop and the death of my sister, and so would continue the evil unless (and his breath filled the room, sweet and forbidden, and the night embraced us all) all words, all actions, forever, by all the family were dedicated to the vindication of the sin, and then that night went and another came, and the sun came out and then it fell, and the nights were black, and all sat kneeling before the cross praying, and there must be no laughter, no happiness, (and so I must forget the setting of the sun and the coming of night with a soft sigh, and I must forget the clouds forming a storm, and I must forget the rain on the leaves, because the sin must be forgiven, because the world is a sad lonely place), and all lives must be dedicated to the god of the evil serpent that had crossed the

---

[21]A Catholic period of prayer lasting nine consecutive days.

path of my father (doomed, that serpent, said the h-man, because in another life that spirit, then in a body, had, like the man my father but unvindicated, found an individual happiness in the small world of self, which is evil, because only god is omnipotent and all those like us must toil forever until death and then the soul will be cleansed and it shall return to the god who is both the god of the Catholic people who have come with images of the saints and the god too of the ancient people, which is the sun, to whom were offered the young warriors, but now it must be prayer offered, and candles nightly). And I grew in shadows because there was infinite silence and no laughter, and one day much later the *h-menob* came again and he looked at me and he said I was a woman (I, who had seen but twelve years) and I must have a mate, and he went I knew to the strange boy who had long ago come to our village, that boy who had stood one day staring at our people, standing against the sun like an ancient warrior who would once have been sacrificed to the god-sun, and in our village an old woman and her husband who longed for a child took him and raised him as their son, so that the boy grew with them, until the man died leaving the woman staring into the sky, and the boy worked in the *milpa*, strangely, many said, for they told how he dug into the earth ruthlessly with bare hands, not allowing the *h-menob* near his land, never making the sacred offer to the winds, never kneeling to the gods, never erecting the small field altar, and they said he would stare at the sky as if seeing there some great being, and his eyes would flash anger like the sea crashing against the rocks, and then he would return, they said, to the digging, the clawing, the tearing with bare hands until they bled, and always he would come to the woman fading into nothing staring into the sky, so that the women of the village shuddered and thought of the infinite justice of god who knew his reasons for the taking of the woman's husband, and they marveled at his goodness because he had not left the woman alone but given her the boy who was like a son, that boy of whom I now heard nightly from the man who came with gifts for my family, saying that the evil of pride was the boy's also, as once it had been of my father, and that I must bring that boy humility—coming nightly, that man, to speak finally of me and the boy, although I could not speak to him—until many days later when we knelt before the cross listening to the words of the priest and wondering what it meant, the marriage, and hearing of pride and humility and the gift of negation, the unturbulence and the peace, eternity . . . And I was silent, because still there must be no joy, and he took me into the house, where once the old man who had loved this boy, now my husband had lived, and the woman who had cared for him like a mother was there still sitting on the floor all night gazing at the sky, sitting there after the other people had left, sitting there while the boy carried me to the hammock, he trembling who was only a boy, trembling like myself, because I must drown all happiness and feel humility, because the tremor that was so glorious must be a sin, because the body pressed against mine, so hard, so tight, so close, so perfect, must be evil, because the flower of my body was opening like the sky opening when night ends its dark sadness and the day comes flooding in bright glory, and yet the present was now—the hammock, the man, my body— now—and I was carried in the waves of passion, and the night moaned coming in through the window, leaving the stars naked, leaving the woman staring outside into the moonless dark, and in that moment, clinging to the body of the boy pressed against mine, I knew sheer beauty lying there in the hammock feeling what the man my father had felt once long ago near the path where the cross stands, what he had felt and for which he must pay, and we, because of the sin, and I must pay for because of the happiness, which was now. . . . And so I wept when it was over, when the fluid had spilled into the opened flower, when the flower had closed carrying the seed of this boy, when it was over and the body beside me felt cold, and I wanted to run away, back to the house where the men and the women would be kneeling and praying to the god, where they would kneel in the darkness and pray for salvation, which I was sacrificing in happiness, which is the greatest evil, which is the greatest sin.

So the flower must close forever and happiness must never come, so the passion must be drowned and the silence prevail, so the seed must smother in the sin itself, that it might never flower in my womb, and so it was I spoke to god in the church and wept because of the sin (but remembered still the fusing bodies, the moment of bursting, of not-isolation, the moment when the seed of life fell and the flower closed embracing it serenely—but it must drown, but it must smother), weeping and promising never to feel that passion again, never again the happiness, but he, the boy, my husband, did not understand the vindication for the sin, and still he took me even as I moaned because I was drowning, wallowing in the passion which I must not feel, which I prayed not to feel and which still filled me, and so I prayed, Forgive me, forgive the sin, turn my body into stone, drown the ecstasy, make my body cold and lifeless, and nightly I tried to hate the man and his body, and nightly the passion recurred, until the hatred came and coldness, the turning of my body into stone, until the happiness was driven away, as the sin must be driven out, until I lay in the hammock feeling only revulsion and hatred for the sin which was in him, and he shouted to me and he cried and pled, but my body was dead finally, and I spoke of god and the serpent and of the burned crop, of death and of my dead sister, of vindication, of sin, and the man cried that god was a stone face he had killed once long ago although it had not died, and so again the sin, and the hating, and the drowning of passion and the hating of sin, of the sad lonely man who was my husband and did not know humility, who toiled the field hating the gods, who must have justice, so that I prayed for justice, for the vindication of sin in the destruction of his crop, for the coming of the rain early that the field might be soaked before the burning of the brush, prayed for the annihilation of that man whose body once I had loved, who did not know humility, who was still a boy, prayed for justice in the house where the woman who had taken the boy as a son sat always by the window staring into the sky and then (but I must not remember, I must forget, this—yet I remember, oh, god, this) the turning in my body, in the secret womb, and the realization that the seed had not smothered in those moments of passion before my body had died, because the seed was his and his the sin, his the cursing of god whom he hated, as I hated the movements within me and the child forming there in myself, trembling because it was already lost, bred by sin and of sin, his child, not mine, for his was the seed, for my body was dead, and I did not tell him of the child, and once I asked the silent woman who sat by the window thinking of the past, asked her the secrets which she must have known, for she had never given birth, Tell me, old woman, tell me the secrets, tell me. And she turned so horrible, and the mouth trembled and the silence was unbroken and she seemed to see me for the first time ever, to understand, and she shrieked, Lost, lost, lost, and then a long-echoing whisper almost nothing, Death. . . . And that was all, forever, because that night, still sitting by the window staring into the night as she had sat it seemed forever, her breathing stopped and the heart stopped beating, and with an amulet of the holy virgin crushed in her tightened fist and with open eyes and a smile so foreign to her face, serene and at peace, she died, and the window remained there framing the piece of her blackness, and the words remained in that lonely dark house, Lost, lost, lost . . . death.

Death came, but in my body life was being born, forming another body, which I began to feel now breathing inside me, forming ineluctably fed by sin, but I, I was drowning in that very sin, although I prayed nightly and burned the candles, but my body grew, so that the boy who was now a man understood one day coming from his *milpa*, and he embraced me hard and the hatred roared within me, and I lunged at him with my nails, ripping his face, and he stood as if understanding now, and then I was weeping because of the past, because of the inevitability, because of the hatred and the love lost, because of the closed flower, because of the loneliness, the isolation, because of the man who stared at me for once with understanding as he raised me gently, gently as on that first night so long ago dead, raised me and carried me to the hammock, walking out afterwards into the not yet setting sun, walking I knew to the field, where he would sleep and remain for days while the child grew within me, and I felt tenderness, which is the remains of lost ecstasy, of dead passion, feeling, once, that sin could not exist, and yet that was sin itself, the trying to answer riddles as my father once, trying to be greater than the god, and so I wept and the child breathed inside and time passed, the days of the long novenas and of the chanting *h-menob*, the holy days of the saints, the days of the abstinence, of the prayers that I longed to pray with the others, with the holy men, but which I dared not because I carried in me the fruit of evil, because I was unclean, but I must not even listen, although the prayers came in the words of the flourishing race, so clear, *Santa María, madre de Dios, ruega señora por nosotros los pecadores, ahora y en la hora de nuestra muerte.* Yes, pray for us sinners but not for the evil, praying not for the birth of evil, which I carried. And finally the days of rejoicing in the village, of the music, that night, hearing the music and singing and chanting, laughter, happiness that must be denied because of the sin, seeing the furious lights bursting, the singing and the ceremony and the loud music, the religious frenzy, the fire, the furiousness, the fever, and inside, the loneliness, the sin, the hatred, the passion long lost, the evil life forming, so that I laughed, covering my ears to drown the sound of happiness which I must not share, which I must hate, and then, and then, and then (no, not this), then the mad beating with my hands to kill the child inside, beating myself where the child was forming, screaming now, beating the child in order to stop the life, to kill the hated evil, the sin of defiance and unhumility, bringing vindication through its death, and all sound ceased except the pounding of my blood, and the man was shaking me until the laughter stopped, until the people outside came running in, until my eyes closed, until again there was peace, blackness, silent sleep . . . but only momentarily, for in the morning, lying in the hammock, I knew the life inside me was still growing, because now I felt the child turn as if in vengeance, felt the tiny body twist defiantly, because it must hate me inevitably even before birth. And still when the woman who stayed in the house watching me slept, still when the man was gone to the *milpa*, still I ran outside feeling the knives of pain stab my womb as I ran along the thorny land, wanting to hear the child weep and know that it had died, falling finally exhausted, screaming because the pain was unbearable, writhing on the ground, until night came and I could hear the sounds of the jungle animals and I saw two deer, mother and child both one, and then the people found me and brought me back, until I grew thin as if the child was squeezing the life from me, until I lay day after day watching the gray moon through the death-window, thinking of the peaceful darkness and longing for serenity, trying not to fall asleep because if I slept, the life would run from me to feed his child, the evil, the sin, and I wanted to stand all night with eyes open even when the invisible knives stabbed me and the pain burned—feeling the twisting, kicking, the beating of the tiny heart inside the womb, until finally, in triumph, leaving me defeated and lost, it came, a tiny girl, and as if in mockery (for I had lost, and so no vindication, only the growing sin), the child wailed full of life as the women held it and smiled, and I knew that it was well, that the hatred with which I had thought to smother it had been its life's blood, that, resisting, it had grown stronger, that the seed had been planted, fed, guarded by evil, that the ancient woman who had long ago sat by the window had looked into the future, for I knew we were lost, the child, the man, myself, all, all lost, as I looked out the window, like the woman of the ancient world, now dead.

And the man loved the girl, and they said in the village that he had found peace, for they saw him in the *milpa* no longer ripping the earth with hatred but planting the corn serenely now, and they spoke, I knew, of me, whispering about the silence in my house, about the girl who must find a mother in the woman who came daily to feed her, because they did not understand the evil and saw only that the child was beautiful, and sometimes— in weakness—I longed to take the tiny thing in my arms, to bring it to my breast and feed it with my own life, to feel the head pressed between my breasts, and I longed to watch it move in the hammock, to cover it when it wept, but the revulsion seized me, and the love was drowned, and I ached with such desire that I ran to the church and knelt weeping, because god must understand, because no matter the desire, I must remain clean, cleansed of the ancient evil, although they walked away from me in the village—as they had walked away from the man, as they would walk away soon from the girl—although I spoke only to my father and my mother, who understood, who went once with me to the place where the snake of evil had touched my father's feet, by the cross that marks the entrance to our village, all three of us kneeling and praying, and then my father hung a tiny effigy of a *santo*[22] on the tree over the cross, and we crossed ourselves, and at the foot of the cross was the skeleton of an agouti which had been there long ago, and we returned to the village, and still I longed to hold the child, until once I succumbed, one angry night with the sky roaring, so that the child cried, even then like a sad lonely lost soul, and I put my hands to my ears not to hear, but still I could hear the sobbing and I felt the aloneness of the motherless child, and I went to the hammock, because the man was not there, and I held the child and kissed its face, hoping desperately that it could return to my womb, crawl there and hide from what must surely come, and that I could return to the womb of my father, that neither she the child nor I the mother had been born, but both had remained in the darkness like a planted seed which does not flower, hoping that my body could embrace hers, that another body could embrace mine, both in peace and without the knowledge of evil, and in that way time would pass the evil, and purity would remain and the flower would not blossom and death would come without the toil of life, thinking that as the tiny mouth searched for the warm milk, as the hands pressed my flesh, and I held my breast to the searching mouth and felt life rushing joyously from me, and there was no longer the child's crying, and I was protected strangely by the searching hands and the clinging mouth—which was the sin, oh, god, the sin, thinking that and yet feeling, *This is happiness, this is love, this is the only purification, this the un-sin,* until I fell asleep on the moist ground, my arms about the child, until I woke up startled with the sun

---

[22]A saint.

in my face, seeing the woman who came daily to feed the child standing smiling at me, and I rose from the ground and silently, as people bury their dead resignedly, I took the child to the woman and laid her in her arms, and touched it for the last time ever, and so I wandered beyond the village then, not knowing why, seeking the jungle animals who hunted the small deer without guilt, seeking those who ran beside the great ones, finding the only peace I knew. And the girl was growing while I wandered far from the village daily after I had lighted the candles to god, wandered even when it rained, because I must not see her, the sin, and time swept past and the girl grew like a strange flower, and she ran wildly to the fields with the man daily, so that the *h-menob* spoke to the man of the sin of the godless child, but the man did not listen, and those men spoke to me, but I would not listen, because if that girl was mine, mine would be the sin, and so she grew with her father, staying with him when the sounds of the animals warned the *milperos* and they had to keep vigil over the corn, and the girl, raised in darkness, in the silence of his house, did not know me, could not know me, although she saw me daily, although she knew I had given birth to her, and she did not even hate me, I felt, and sometimes she would talk to me, when she was still childlike once in the church when she would have touched me, and I longed to touch her, but I did not, and so she spoke to her father, who loved her, who watched her as her body began to flower toward maturity, who saw in the child the girl that would soon be, who loved her as perhaps he had loved me once in the dead past, who watched her grow those thirteen years and then another, and another, until it was fifteen years since I had lain hoping she would come dead from my womb, fifteen years of her life, and she was, oh, more beautiful than the virgin to whom I prayed daily, glorious for her father, who found in her the unrealized past, and she the girl was strange, running into the field laughing recklessly like the wind, and I knew that she loved her father as an animal loves, from necessity, because I felt—knew—that the love he gave her was the love I had denied, so that on those nights in the field he lay with her as I had lain with him, loving in her I knew not the found daughter but the lost wife, myself, and I wondered if that girl knew the same ecstasy I had known, the same revulsion later, wondered if the sin had been so powerful that somehow she would understand without knowing, and I prayed for vindication still, for the destruction of the field, and later when I saw the happiness of the man who was my husband I prayed too for the loss of the girl, that again he would be alone, as I was alone, and sad, and we did not speak, all silent, walking silently like secret shadows in that house of the thundering silence.

And then the boy came.

And the serenity that the man had found in his daughter, the serenity which had made him forget the stone face of the angry god, that serenity was gone forever.

Again the ruthless digging into the earth, again the loathing and the turbulence now that the secret boy of the mystery had come, because he realized, that man, my husband, the father, that the girl would never be his again, that his happiness had fled into the vast sky which he searched again with asking eyes.

And I realized the justice, the vindication for his sin, and so even in the defeat, even in the loneliness I had prayed for, even in that, there was triumph, for me, for the god.

And she, the girl, she too who was gone then one day (only yesterday, but the past is a vast plain and yesterday is as irretrievable, as lost, as dead, as hopelessly buried as the very beginning of time), she must fade now for me into the dark chambers of memory, and she had begun her futile search for the strange boy of the desperate eyes.

For she will never find him.

For she will search and search (as the man has searched vainly, as I have searched vainly through the labyrinthine life).

But she will never find him, that girl to whom I gave life.

She will never find the boy of the longing eyes.

4

The tortillas rested beside her now, brown, and the fire for cooking had gone out. The woman held the round tortillas in her gaunt hands. She extended them silently to her husband.

He took them, putting in them the beans, and he folded the tortillas, and he ate quietly.

Quickly, the woman turned from him, looking at the empty hammock of the girl through the blur of the tears in her eyes.

FIVE: The Boy

I

And who was this boy that the girl searched, that the man hated, that the woman prayed for?

He was a strange, mysterious, lonely, secret, desperate boy who had come to this village of the girl quite by accident, quite strangely.

For in this country, in the upper part, about the interior, beyond where the men grew corn, into the land where the *chicle* is, closer to civilization and the modern cities, beyond this are the *henequén* plantations, where the hemp is grown. Here live the very rich people, who come from the angry cities, sometimes beyond the sea, who come to live on these plantations only for a short time. Then they return to the cities, among their own people, perhaps no farther away than the harbor city, where life never pauses, or perhaps to the capital of that state, or to the capital of the country itself. They come here, most of them, to seek a kind of serenity in a kind of isolation. For this state is separated on one side from the rest of the country, from the capital city of the state, by the *henequén* jungle, the tribal villages set far down into the thorny country, the villages of those of the ancient races who fled from the modern life, beyond the ancient pyramids of the slowly disintegrating races, and separated on the other side by the vast body of water.

And this is how the strange, secret, lonely, mysterious, desperate boy of the yearning eyes came to such a plantation. This is how he came finally to the village of the girl.

2

The capital of the country itself, which is far beyond this state, separated from it by the jungle, is a city, and everywhere are the brilliant restaurants and luxurious cafés, sprawling houses of the rich, rich people, and the streets are crowded with the brilliant cars of the aimless people, and life is an ascending scale of recklessness. And behind all this—behind the richness, the tawdriness, behind the lavishness and wealth—is the squalor, the poverty, the hopelessness, despair and the futility.

Laughter is national, and the sound of the incessantly strumming guitars, but along every street, forming compositely an endless chain, an unlinked tattered necklace, are the beggars with outstretched fingers, cursing and blessing alternately, and the brown, gaunt-faced shawled women surrounded by tiny grotesque children also with hands outstretched, fingers clutching at nothing, and the twisted horrible men with filthy pleading palms, and the old, old women with upward-looking eyes, with parched lips moving in silent prayer.

Almost adjacent to the magnificent buildings are the broken-down shacks often of box-cardboard, where people live who stand daily on street corners selling candy or bread or pottery or wooden toys with strings or false glittering jewelry brightly shining to rival the gleam from the gold-toothed mouths of the leering unbuying customers that parade the streets daily in order to leer.

And in such an area the boy first appeared.

And for him, even as a child, the only real thing was unreality, and he walked the streets peering into extravagant stores, longing and hoping, living for the time to come, and at night he would hear the music coming from the lighted places, floating into the darkness outside like exotic perfume. He grew that way, dreaming, seeking only a means of escaping, and he lived in different houses, in that same neighborhood, where the women fed him when they could, where those women spoke of him in amazement and wondered from where he had come, those very same women who had seen him first as a child nine years old, when he had just appeared one day, alone, not speaking to anyone until much later, retreating from those who neared him like a frightened animal, speaking until much later. Then, when he spoke to them, this child of nine, it was to speak of things which they could not understand, of a beautiful woman, in a beautiful world, in a beautiful house. So they coaxed him, those people who had no other way of escape but through the eyes of this boy, to tell them his stories, and the intense-eyed child would begin weaving the stories endlessly for the desperate people.

Always in these stories there was a woman, who was perfect (Like Mary? asked the women, *como la virgencita santa?*[23]) and the boy nodded, holding in his hand a wooden crucifix tied about his neck with a dirty piece of string and he added Yes, like the sacred virgin, and kind, and loving. And there was also a harsh cruel angry man who both loved and hated the woman, who beat her savagely when he hated her, but the woman loved a child whom the man hated even more, and together, the woman and the boy, they would flee far away, would flee laughing to very far, golden, places until the man found them again, until the beating started all over.

The women and the men listened intently to these stories, of the golden palaces that gleamed like the sun and the stars, and then one day one of the women (on a hot torrid city night,

[23]Like the holy little virgin.

late, when the boy had come back from the streets, when even the older children sat in the moonless night with the small wooden shoeshine boxes resting beside them), asked anxiously, "And what happened to her, what happened to this woman, *chico?*"[24]

The boy sighed.

The silence was long.

He stared far away.

"They came for her one day," he said finally. "And they took her in a black box. And she will never come back again."

He grew up that way, until no one wondered any longer from where he had come, until even the magic of him began to fade for them, until he became for them a liar. He stopped going out with the other boys of the shoeshine boxes. He went alone now, walking through the streets of the very rich, staring at those houses. Occasionally someone would call to him, "*Hola, muchacho,* I would like to have a shine, but usually the boy would not turn, and if he did accept the job, he would usually dirty the man's socks, and so he made very little money. Then he would go with the men when they went to their corners to sell bread or candy or wooden toys with strings or false jewelry. He would stand staring far beyond, and this irritated the men who could not dream, and they cursed the boy loudly, "*Cabrón,*"[25] they said, "*estúpido, desgraciado, maldito, imbécil,*"[26] and they cried, "*lárgate de aquí.*"[27]

One day one of the men whom he helped saw the small crucifix about the boy's neck. It was very like those that the man sold, and he thought the boy was a thief. He lunged angrily at

---

[24]An expression suggesting "boy."

[25]You bastard.

[26]Stupid, unfortunate, evil and imbecile.

[27]Get out of here.

the boy, and the boy sprang back. "*Ladrón,*"[28] the man cried, "*policía,*[29] he has stolen from me. Help me."

People gathered about them quickly, and the man pled with the crowd to help him catch the boy, the boy was a dangerous criminal, look at him. And the boy stood defiantly only a few feet away holding the small crucifix about his neck. But the crowd only looked on, and the man became angrier, his face reddening as he advanced cautiously toward the boy until the two were mere inches apart. Then the man made a desperate lunge, but the boy moved too quickly, and the man fell sprawled on the street. One of the very small children in the crowd kicked the man gleefully.

"*Malagradecido,*"[30] the man wept, shouting at the boy, who still stood defiantly, hands on hips. "Ungrateful one. Robber."

The boy turned away, disappearing around the corner with the wooden crucifix clenched in his hand like a precious jewel.

After that he did not return to those people, and even the women who had seen the crucifix often about the boy's neck, who knew that he had not stolen it, agreed that he would come to no good. If he had not stolen this time, they said, he would surely begin to steal soon from them. Later, they spoke of how he would not work, of how he was too old for dreams, of how he was a liar, of how he was lazy and how he had no ambition to work for his food, and they forgot the child of not so long ago who had sat wide-eyed creating magic for them, spinning the longed-for fascination.

---

[28]Thief.
[29]Police.
[30]Ungrateful.

3

He was fourteen years old.

He worked in restaurants, washing dishes, still dreaming. He would move from place to place, from restaurant to restaurant, café to café. He was not a good worker, they all said, and they let him go often without paying him.

Then he was fifteen years old.

He would walk through the dark streets, listening for the sound of the music coming from inside the bars. Often, he would go into the places where no one noticed his torn dirty clothes, would go in to listen to the music, fascinated, dreaming. Then he would walk outside into the dirty night air, and the music would remain in his mind, recurring not as he had heard it, garish and vulgar, but as a supreme symphony. And the image would spring into his longing mind, the whirling, the lights, the love, the admiration, the applause, the love.

Then he was sixteen.

He was in one of the crowded smoky places listening to the music which his mind would distill of vulgarity, and standing there he could see his own image reflected hundreds of times about the many-mirrored room, behind the bar, against the wall, the tiny dazzling mirrors. He felt dizzy at the thought of himself in so many places. For a moment he wanted to stand in the center of the small dance floor, and then whirl about, seeing the thousand spinning images. But he could not. He must remain in the shadows in the background, because even if he could have bought something, he wanted nothing but to stand there creating for himself another, grand world.

Then he felt someone lay a hand on his shoulder, where his flesh was bare through the torn shirt. His first thought was to run, but when he turned, he saw very close to him the forcedly smiling face of a gray-haired middle-aged man.

"*Hola, muchacho*," said the middle-aged man. His smile was set, fixed there. The fingers on the boy's shoulder were moist, tense. . . . There was a ring on one finger, and it caught the gleam from the lights above, dancing in the boy's eyes.

The boy stared at the ring, fascinated. He had seen the false jewelry that the men sold on street corners, and he had grown to recognize in those stones the cheap impure brightness. The stone on this hand on his shoulder was different.

He smiled at the man, a smile very much still that of a very young boy.

The middle-aged man's fingers clung. The smile tensed like that of someone trying to conceal emotion, turmoil. The middle-aged man said, "You are alone?" He spoke in a secretive, accented voice. He was perhaps not of this country. He had not removed his hand. It rested fixed like the smile.

"Yes," the boy said quickly, his eyes still on the ring.

The man noticed the boy's gaze. "Do you like this ring?" he said quickly. "It is very pretty, isn't it?"

"Yes," the boy said. "*Sí, mucho.*"

The middle-aged man laughed, the tenseness, not so apparent now, the smile relaxing, not set so firmly now. He removed his hand finally from the boy's shoulder, cautiously, hesitantly. But he still stared intently at the boy. The boy met his gaze. The man dropped his eyes quickly.

"It is beautiful," the boy said noticing how the light played on it.

"Listen," hissed the man in one breath. "Listen," he hissed. "Listen," he said, as if that was the only word he could form.

A man brushed against the boy and the man. The middle-aged man looked away quickly, his face almost collapsing, expressionless. Then the intruder was gone.

Again the hoarse, nervous, anxious, hissing voice, again the same word, as if it was all he dare say, "Listen."

"It is a beautiful ring," the boy said.

"Do you want it?" the man said finally. "Do you think it is wonderful? Do you want it?"

A thin painted woman passed the two. She eyed them both, and then she laughed, staring at the man laughing.

"Come with me then," said the man, "and I will give you the ring." He spoke fast, as if afraid of his own silence now. "If you want it."

"Yes," the boy said.

Outside, the man summoned a taxi, and they got in. "I will give you the ring if you really want it," the middle-aged man whispered to the boy.

The house where they went was glorious, and the boy stood looking at it, at the elaborate, jewel-splendor of it. Yes, it was to a house much like this that he had come with the woman of his stories. To a house like this where they had sought refuge from the angry man. It was of this that he had spoken, of the graceful drapes like dancers swaying with the breeze, here that they had danced before the mirrors gilded, golden. Beyond reality, the tall windows and the soft floors.

Now the smile was gone completely from the man's face. Now the face that had seemed artificial in the unreal light of the bar was harshly real, crumpled, real even beyond middle-age, and sad and pained, an ugly, lonely, pained face.

But the boy did not see that. His eyes saw, as he stood in that dazzling illumined room his own reflection, his own image as if he were someone else standing there. And he smiled, spinning about like a child with a precious toy.

The man of the crumpled face had a bottle in his hand, and a glass which he held out to the boy. But the boy did not even see the proffered glass. The man drank from the bottle feverishly.

"Yes," he said as if to himself, looking at the boy, "yes, you are very handsome and . . . and . . . " He sighed, sat down, the bottle in his hand. "Here," he said, extending the ring to the boy. "This is what you came for. I am always foolish, even now, even after all these times, foolish to believe that . . . to hope that . . . Yes," he repeated, "and you are so handsome. And I, I am . . . I am so . . . " He stopped abruptly again, choking the words with the liquor, closing his eyes, shutting out his reality. "Here, take the ring."

The boy held it tightly in his hand, as if believing that if he released his grip, the man would reclaim it.

"It is yours," said the gray-haired man. Then he drank from the bottle once again long, again urgently. He wiped his forehead. "I am choking," he said. Then he was looking at the boy, with anger. "But what do you care about me?" he shouted. "What do you know about loneliness?" Covering his face, "Oh, god," he said, "over and over, night to night, then night again—desiring—oh god, why don't I die? Why am I such a coward?"

He smiled, an unhappy smile. "Do you want to know why? Because I am foolish to believe, to hope that some day, even now, somehow, there will be someone who . . . " His hands rose to his face again covering it. Then he began to cough, as if choking, his eyes closed, the bottle turned down, the liquor spilling.

"God, god, god."

The boy had not moved. He was aware of the man's voice but he was not listening to him. The ring seemed to burn in his hand. It was a tiny fire sparkling like a flame. He closed his eyes, seeing himself in that astonishing house. Then he began to laugh, loudly, joyously.

The man sprang from the chair. His hands grasped the boy harshly. "Are you laughing at me?" he shouted.

The boy clung to the ring, his eyes wide and desperate. "It is mine," he shouted back. "You gave it to me." He held the ring behind him in a fist.

The man released him.

"I will not take it from you," he sighed. "I only thought you were laughing at me. . . . But no," he said, shaking his head dazedly, "you were not even listening." He smiled wryly. "And why should you care, you who are handsome and . . . " He looked down at the floor, where the liquor had spilled, and this time he was able to finish, " . . . and young." He sighed at last. "Oh," he cried, "if I could take your youth, your face, your body, if I could drain them from you."

He was still looking at the boy, but now no longer furtively, now very openly desiring.

"I will not take the ring from you," he said in a hoarse resigned voice.

After that the boy remained there with the man. He went with him everywhere, pointing to the things he wanted, which the man bought. For the boy it was like living in the golden world he had spoken of so often. Soon he began to notice with pleasure, filling his greatest need, the admiring glances he received.

Later, in the house, in the bedroom which was his, he would whirl about the room, the small wooden crucifix—which he would not give up even for more expensive ones—spinning about his neck. The music he had heard would pass automatically through his mind. His hands would run down his body, which was lithe and supple. He would touch his face, which was finely contoured, sensually masculine, and he would be aware of himself, acutely aware. He would remember, treasure, all the admiring furtive glances. But strangely he did not want any of these people who admired him, neither the young nor the old like the man with whom he stayed. Instead, he felt contempt almost like revulsion for them, and yet he remembered every glance he received, every whisper, locking up these memories needfully as a person stores food to keep from starvation.

Yet there were times now when that was not enough. If he had seen a smile which he thought contemptuous, if he had noticed a look which he thought critical, if he had overheard a comment which he thought adverse—if he had not been looked at—he would run frantically, very unsure of himself and deeply wounded. He would feel the uncertainty welling within him, the futility, the hopelessness. Then his hands would rise automatically to touch his face, and then the assurance would return as suddenly as it had left him.

As time passed, he would stay longer and longer in his room, for hours sometimes. At certain times he would not be able to face the others, not even the man, and he would dread leaving the house. He remained in that one room for hours sometimes, alone, playing the music the man had bought for him, standing sometimes watching the record turn around and around and his own outline silhouetted in the glossy-black middle-surface. Other times he would improvise movements, twisting his body in a dance. Finally, he would fall exhausted on the bed laughing nervously, his hands about himself.

Once the man of the crumbling face came into the room when the boy was dancing.

"Look," the boy shouted. "Look at me." Then he came toward the man, and his eyes were urgent and longing, frantic, pleading. "I want to dance," he said. "Will you help me? I want to be a dancer."

The record was still on the table. It was a *bolero*.[31] The boy had to shout to be heard.

"Look at me," he shouted. "Do you think I will be a great dancer? Look at me. Look."

"Yes," the man said.

"Only yes?" the boy said. "I will be great, I will be the greatest dancer in all the world, they will all love me, they will all shout for me, they will all admire me. Oh, I will dance and dance. I will be the greatest dancer in all the world."

He ran to the table, where the bolero had stopped. He reached for the record, spinning himself recklessly. Then he flung the record against the wall, drowning the ensuing crashing with a desperate shout like a moan.

There were times, however, when the boy would not remain inside that house, when the need for others became urgent in him. Such times he would long for the people, and then usually they would go to the theater, most often to the dance. The boy would watch the movements hungrily. Then back in the dazzling house he would be depressed, silent, not even speaking to the man.

As the relationship proceeded, the man became possessive.

He would no longer go out, even to the theater. At night, he would drink. The abuse would recur, the accusations, the harsh recriminations. Then he would cry. He would praise the boy, his loyalty, begging him never to leave him, promising to take him wherever he wanted to go, speaking of the perfect contentment which he had found at last after years of searching from young man to young man, desiring each for short periods only, hating them afterwards.

"But not you," he told the boy.

Still, the next day, he would be watching the boy to see that he did not leave the house, refusing him money in order that he would not leave, until, finally, when the possessiveness had become overwhelming, when the fear of loneliness was unbear-

---

[31] A ballad love song.

able, the man told the boy enthusiastically, one day, that they would go on a trip, far away, where the boy would have everything, where everything would be perfect.

"Perfect," he said, and even the crumpling face seemed happy all at once. "Perfect," he said.

And so they traveled by airplane the next day, the boy excited and on the brink of something new and wonderful.

Then they were in a city, in another state, not so big, so beautiful, so lavish, as the other from which they had come. Still, it was exciting for the boy, because they stayed in a large hotel, where the people looked at him admiringly, where he drank their admiration urgently.

The next day, they set out by train, into the interior of that state. Finally, they reached the man's *henequén* plantation, where there were only the natives that cared for the land, only the strange Indians, where the man, like others, thought to find serenity, escape from the turbulence in a kind of isolation.

At first the boy was very happy. It was different, this place. There was a different kind of lavishness, the kind of lavishness which he had never explored even with the woman of his stories.

It was hot here. The sun burned furiously. And the boy's skin turned brown, and his eyes looked lighter than ever, and this pleased him very much. But here there was only the man to notice him, and the boy became slowly melancholy. He was still very young then, only sixteen, and as time passed in that plantation, there came a restlessness in him, an urgency which the man recognized but could not understand, accept. When the man was not in the house, the boy spent most of his time in the giant bedroom, so that one day, coming early from the tour over the plantation, over the surrounding land, the man began to wonder what particular fascination the room held for the boy.

He walked into that room of the boy, which he had seen many, many times.

The boy was outside then, the man could see him through the window, and he could see him staring into the far, far distance.

The man's eyes traveled over the boy's room. Nothing to reveal the boy's fascination, nothing but the lavish, ludicrously elaborate furniture which the boy himself had chosen, nothing, not even the records, which had been left behind purposely by the man. No, nothing but the furniture which the boy had chosen in the capital, the soft bed, the drapes that became graceful dancers when the wind blew and the dazzling mirrors arranged like a parody altar on top of two platform-steps.

The man's image was reproduced three times at different angles in those mirrors, and as he moved closer, those multiplied. And he thought, *In those mirrors there are many selves, many images, and so the tragedy is not one only but many times as great as if I were less than one, or nothing.*

With a deep sigh, he turned quickly from them. Still he could not understand. So he stood in that room of the dazzling altar-mirrors but he did not understand, would not know, standing there wondering.

Outside, the boy gazed at his own shadow. Then he turned, twisting his body as if he were dancing before an admiring audience. He smiled then, as he seldom smiled now with the man, even at the breathtaking wealth which was that man's.

Then one day, months later when the boy was older, when he was seventeen, when the urgency was overflowing, when the restlessness was unbearable, one day he told the man (as they sat in electric tension, at the long lavish white table, with the sun-browned Indians serving the food, and the long graceful drapes swaying rhythmically with the wind which was oppressively hot, and the sound of the voices of the plantation workers floating into the room serenely from the outside,) that he must return to the city.

The man would not agree. At first, he was kind, kinder than he had been for a long time. He promised the boy more riches, more grandeur if he would remain. He would send for the records so that the boy could dance again as much as he wanted. The boy did not answer, but in a few days, new records came.

Time passed in almost-silence. Still, the boy longed for the city. He retreated into his room, remaining there, playing the music incessantly.

Once the man came early to the house. He heard the music, loud, filling the house savagely. He went to the room where the boy was, thinking of the young whirling body. He heard laughter coming from within, the boy's familiar nervous laughter, heard it even above the sound of the passionate music, which was loud and fierce. He opened the door cautiously, without knowing why.   Then he saw the boy.

The boy was in the center of the room, whirling, dancing there before the three mirrors. As he moved, his hands traveled obscenely down his body. And he was completely naked except for the crucifix about his neck tied with the dirty piece of string. His hair had fallen over his forehead, and the longing eyes were transformed, were slanted, and his mouth was parted, and he looked strange and evil and cruel—and beautiful to the man. Then the boy's arms tightened about himself in a passionate embrace, and all movement stopped. He, himself and the images reflected in the mirrors stood staring at each other. His eyes closed, slowly, and the arms tightened urgently.

Quickly, the man closed the door. He stood leaning against it, breathing hard, feeling the perspiration running down his body.

The incident was not mentioned by the man, and the boy was not aware that the man had seen him.

And so their lives continued, and the possessiveness became hungrier in the man, and again the recriminations. He spoke of the selfishness of the boy, of his ingratitude. But always he would finish by weeping and begging the boy never to leave him, speaking of his own unselfish love for the boy.

Then again the boy told the man that they must return to the city, pled with the man, told him that he was burning here in this place, that he would die if they did not return. The man became hysterical, screaming at the boy, and his face collapsed with rage as he shouted with wild hysteria, and his hands trembled with the thought of the coming loneliness. He wept, that man, he hurled accusations, finally pleading as he had pled so many times

"Look at me," he shouted at the boy. "Look at my face. I am . . . old. The world keeps whirling recklessly past me, swiftly, with time, and I remain behind. I cannot go with it. I must remain clinging. . . . To what? Tell me. To nothing? Do you know what nothing is? The whirling void, the black vacuity, the labyrinthine nothingness, the vortex, the spinning emptiness? The nothing. Can you know? You who have no heart, who cannot love, you who have never known loneliness, you whom I created from nothing, who have never loved, whom I picked from the filth. And what have you returned? What have you given? Again, the empty, vacuous nothing that pursues me like time?"

He sobbed, still trembling, but the tears were no longer coming, only the spasmodic sobs, anxious, desperate, afraid.

"Do you know about the substitution for love?" he cried. "Do you know about the isolation, the haven which I searched and thought I had found at last here with you? Do you know about the others like you who have breezed through my life in the cities of that world beyond this house? Can you know what it is to search in the emptiness and think, I have found it, only to realize, I have lost it? And so in this world of you and myself, away from the other lives and the pursuers' accusations, I thought at last there was peace. Again, I have found it, only to realize I have lost it? No, no."

He stood very close to the boy now, whispering at first, then his voice rising, "What is it you want? What more can I give you? Look at yourself now. Remember yourself as you were before I brought you with me, before I . . . Remember the filth, the rot. Remember this, and tell me you want to return to it, to lose all this? Have you forgotten so quickly?"

Now he moved away from the boy. Now he stood by the window looking out, saying, "Through the dark world they say man must search. But for what?" He faced the boy. "For those like you, those evil ones like you, who must hurt? And why must you hurt?" he pled. "What have I done? Oh, god, why am I damned?"

He sobbed into his hands, sobbing without tears, which had long been exhausted.

And the boy did not move. He remained silent, watching the drapes dancing with the wind, seeing, then, on the floor, his own shadow from the burning candles, his own swaying shadow, gracefully like a ghost not of the past but of the future.

Then the man, in one urgent gasp, shouted, "What do you want?"

And then slowly his face became distorted diabolically, his features hidden in the maze of wrinkles.

"Do you want a mother?" he shouted. "The mother lost in the filth, the mire? A mother?" he screamed.

The images of the dancing figures—of the swaying shadows, of the shifting drapes—exploded in the boy's mind.

"Shut up," the boy shouted, his fists threatening. "Shut up."

And the man was laughing shrilly, hysterical, "A mother? A mother? A mother?"

Silence then, and silent recriminations again, silent accusations, and the desperate wounded selves, silently. The boy still longed to return to the city, longed for it with intensity as he walked in the eternity of the scorching afternoons outside, alone staring at his shadow, sighing lonesomely as the sun set at last, leaving him one and alone without even a shadow, without the other, the complement self. And he seldom spoke to the man, and he remained outside often, and he slept very troubled in the mirrored room.

And the man lay in his room and he did not sleep. He lay in the hovering darkness and heard the sinister shouts from the ghosts of the past. And he was remembering the accusations, the pleading, the screaming, and he longed for the boy.

One day, the boy thought, *I will run away*. He repeated easily to himself, *Yes, I will run away*.

He did not think of obstacles, did not think he did not know this country, but he remembered only the train that had brought them here from the outside world, and he remembered that they had not traveled long to get to the plantation.

I will run away. Tomorrow. Tomorrow I will run away.

That night he was pleasant to the man, and the man responded with intensity. The man felt again the evasive happiness return, the un-isolation.

The next day the boy was gone.

Certain, because he was very young, that he would find the place where the train would carry him back to the city from which he would return to the other state from which he had come, the boy walked farther and farther, realizing, much later, that he was lost.

Now he reached a group of thatch houses, where the people were friendly, where they pointed out the way to him, but then to another village, where the people would know, they said (speaking in the Spanish which was all that bound them to the outside world of the flourishing race), the direction of that world.

So the boy walked on and on, encountering more and more often the small hidden villages circling the crude *cenote*, which was for water, and the boy would eat there, when the people were friendly, but often he would have to flee, feeling the hostility, traveling farther into the interior, through the thickness, until he reached another village, a larger one, and the boy was tired then, and exhausted, and afraid.

And he had reached the village of the girl, of the man, the village of the woman.

4

He stood silhouetted against the sun of the sultry morning.

I will never reach the city, he thought. *I am lost. I will wander and wander and I will never reach the city.*

His clothes were torn at various places, where low-hanging branches had clawed at his flesh. Over his forehead he held a straw hat given to him in another village, but even standing so, unmoving, he could feel no relief from the heat. His body seemed submerged in a pool of angry steam, and he squinted, trying to focus his eyes.

In this village I will eat and drink, he thought resignedly, *and sleep perhaps, and then I will leave, and perhaps then there will be another village, where perhaps I will not stay because they will not want me, and then another and another village, until perhaps there will be no more. But I will never find the city now. I am lost. I am hopelessly lost.*

He saw someone moving toward him.

He could not tell whether it was a man or a woman, even a child. Everything before him converged into a haze because he faced the sun. As the person moving toward him came closer, taking form slowly, he saw the girl.

She was dark and her hair was black and long but tightly braided, and her eyes were slanted slightly and a brown that was almost yellow, and her cheekbones were high and she was very, very beautiful, and her skin was soft brown and her lips sensual, very red and her body was very beautiful, and she was very, very young, younger even than the boy, who was very young, who was only seventeen, who stood now looking at her.

The sun burned into the boy's mind scorching all memory, and he stood like one hypnotized seeing nothing now but the furious ball of flaming white sun above.

"I want water," he sighed. "I am thirsty, hungry. I am lost."

The girl did not move, did not speak. She merely watched him.

"Do you understand?" he asked without anger, or even impatience, only tired. "Do you understand that I am very thirsty?"

She did understand, understood well the words of the Mexican people, learned from her father the long afternoons. But still she did not speak, still did not move, still did not respond, still remained watching.

He passed his hand over his forehead. The bleached hat fell to the ground, and the sun fell on him scorching. He sighed. Then he began to walk away from the girl, feeling the sun pierce the torn clothes, feeling drops of perspiration streak his face.

The girl walked behind him. Then, as he proceeded still slowly but faster than before, she moved more rapidly. Once, as he seemed about to fall, she gave a gasp because perhaps already she had formed in her mind the before-then undreamed dream, dreaming it now as she followed him with less uncertainty, almost walking beside him now, until once again ready to fall, he turned to her in supplication, "I am thirsty," and she walked next to him, leading him now to the house of her father.

When they had reached it, he sat on the shaded ground. He was sheltered from the furious sun by the small thatch house.

Two small boys ran past the house. They stopped abruptly, watching the intruder to their village, who looked strange and unlike them. They moved on hurriedly.

The girl still stared at him, wanting very much to touch him. Then she looked away from the boy, looked once inside the house, through the door, and she saw her mother watching them, the gaunt thin Indian woman. The mother turned away.

The boy looked at the girl pleadingly. He was hardly able to speak. Then he saw the mother, who had come outside word-lessly walking down the path, down the dirty road—a shadow, barefooted—walking toward the church.

At last, the girl had gone into the house. At last, she came out and she had water for the boy, and food, and he reached urgently after the water. Then, afterwards, more slowly, he ate the food, and asked for more, which he ate even more slowly, treasuring the taste.

As he ate, the girl still watched him.

Then he had finished.

Then he sat there wordlessly, exhausted, but satisfied. The sun was not so hot and the shade was darker, cooler. Then they remained there silently.

And then the woman returned, walking past her daughter, walking past the boy wordlessly, walking inside the house, like one long dead but still unburied, still hopelessly breathing, a shadow.

The boy felt the strength returning to him slowly. He was looking anxiously about him. Now he could think clearly again. The sun would set soon, and it would be night, and dark, and then he would not be able to walk, even if these people could show him the way to the place that would take him to the city, even if this girl would lead him there, even then he would not be able to walk. He would have to sleep tonight, because he was very tired and had to rest. *Tomorrow* . . .

"There is a great city away from here," he told her, motioning with his hands, still uncertain that she understood him. "But nearer here there is a place where a train will carry me to another city, from where I can go away, where I must. Do you understand me?"

"Yes," she said.

"I must find it," he said, feeling the urgency return with strength. "Can you tell me where that place is, where I will take the train to the city?" He was looking at her, pleading with her to say yes even if she meant no.

She felt the intense pleading, but she felt more acutely her own unhappiness. *He will leave,* she thought, and she was dreaming the just-dreamed dream. *He will leave. And he is asking me to help him.*

"No," she answered at last, her gaze falling guiltily from his face. "There is no such village near here. There is no way."

He reached for her shoulders, desperately. "There is," he insisted. "There is." Then his hands released the girl, and his face changed again to the face of one pleading. "If you help me," he said, "I will give you . . . I will give you . . . " There was nothing in his pockets, which he searched. Then his hands reached for the cross about his neck, and they fell immediately once they had touched the crucifix. "No," he said quickly. He removed the ring which the man had given him. "I will give you this ring," he said.

She turned away.

"Oh, don't you understand? If you will not help me, I will have to wander again, leave tonight perhaps, and wander and wander."

And suddenly she felt a shame she had never felt before, even as she dreamed the dream furiously, wanting to help him so he would not hate her.

"My father will know," she said. Then quickly, regretting it, "No, he will not know," she said. "There is no way to . . . "

But the boy did not even hear her last words, would not believe them. He looked about him anxiously, hoping that magically the man of whom the girl spoke would appear.

"Where is he?" he asked.

Now, a woman passed by, very old and gnarled, and she looked at the girl, then at the boy suspiciously, and she stopped involuntarily when she saw the boy. Then she hurried away, making a hurried sign of the cross.

"Listen," the boy said. "I must see that man now. Will you help me?" He was pleading, but his face was urgent. His hands reached nervously for the small cross about his neck, and he fingered it delicately, twisting it.

"He will come back," the girl said resignedly. "Tonight, perhaps. Perhaps not until tomorrow night. He is in the field, far away," she said.

"Take me there now," he demanded, his eyes searching about him, as if expecting the night to capture him.

She looked away again. "It is too late," she said pointing to the sun sinking. "It is far from here, very, very far. The night is coming. Soon now, it will be dark, and the jungle animals will be searching, and the lonely spirits from the other life will be luring hunters to their death, the night is very black. Look, look at the purple sky, and look, beyond, see the star, it is the first star of the night, and if we go to that field which is very far, we would perhaps get lost, see the star, and over there, another, see it, do you feel the night coming?"

He sighed. "But where will I stay? I must sleep tonight. You do not understand that I am lost, that I have been traveling since . . . since . . . " He had forgotten for how long. He looked at her accusingly as if she were responsible for his plight.

And she too was looking at him, looking long at this boy of the Mexican people, studying him. His skin was brown with the sun, not the color of the earth, and his dark hair was not as dark as that of the men of her village. His eyes were a color she had never seen.

"You can stay here," she said. "You can wait for him here. Tonight. And tomorrow, if he has not returned, I will take you to him, if you want."

"But where will I sleep?" he demanded. "I cannot remain out here. Look, see over there, near your star, those are clouds. It could rain tonight. I cannot stay outside. I am too tired." He looked inside the house longingly, where he could see a hammock by the window.

The girl pointed to a thatched hut in the yard. "It is where the animals slept once," she said, "but all the chickens were killed when my mother's father was dying. You can sleep there," she said.

The boy looked again at the sky, at the cold stars now appearing.

There in the sky the clouds were converging furiously, like enemies, or like lovers in ecstasy, rolling and gray in the darkening sky where the sun had disappeared.

"Yes," he sighed wearily.

"It will shelter you." The girl still looked at him, intensely, and now there was a smile on her face, and the smile was mysterious and secret.

The boy could not sleep.

He lay on the scorched earth with his hands under his head. Through the thatch of the small hut he could see the sky and occasionally, when the converging clouds parted, the moon, which was sad and white, lonely like a forgotten bride. Then the clouds embraced, fused, and the light of the moon was gone, as if the forgotten bride was envious of the ecstasy of the fusing clouds. Now there was only the oppressive heat, and the strange night-sounds over and over in a monotonous rhythm.

Directly above the boy a spider was weaving a web with slow movements. The invisible thread swayed occasionally, and the spider seemed suspended in the air.

Once again the clouds parted, drifted apart like satiated lovers. The moon came out, waving its veils sadly. The stars were cold, buried deep in the sky, and they watched with glittering eyes the dolefully sighing moon.

The boy closed his eyes tightly, putting his hands to his face and turning his head so that the moonlight would not fall on his face. Tonight, as he lay there on the ground of this foreign village the moon troubled him greatly and he did not know why. The light of the sun, which was harsh and unsecret—unashamedly naked—was not accusing like the tenebrous purple of the mourning moon. He longed desperately for the coming of day, and the thought that many hours separated him from the rising of the sun filled him with a sudden stark terror, more horrible because there was no immediate object to fear, only a nameless something hovering outside the hut.

He opened his eyes again, focusing all his attention on the spider. *It is weaving a trap,* he thought involuntarily. And that thought filled him with revulsion, inexplicable fear. He could see himself caught in the mesh of cobwebs, struggling to get out. He could feel the clinging silver threads across his face like a net.

His fingers would try to remove horrible things from his eyes, but they would enshroud him like a tenacious veil.

A breeze entered. The cobwebs swayed.

Like silent dancers, the boy thought, and smiled. *Like silent dancers*, his mind repeated purposely, to expel the fear.

Now he was lying with hands under his head looking up. The moon stared accusingly at him. He shuddered. The sight of the moon seemed to radiate cold, despite the stifling heat in the small thatch hut.

Why do you accuse me? he thought.

The sun is a man burning furiously with life, the boy thought, *but the moon is a veiled woman sighing a requiem of loneliness.* And the boy felt strangely guilty. He turned his face again from the light of the moon.

Then the night was interrupted by the sound of surreptitious footsteps, of feet moving cautiously through the rustling brush outside the hut.

Sitting up, the boy listened intently to the sound. All the previous nameless fears that had filled him with terror fused now, focused on the footsteps, finding an object, and the fear was intensified.

I will never leave this village, the boy thought frantically.

The nameless horror petrified him. The night would collapse like the walls of a cave. The moon would rush through the thatch and scorch him with its frozen fire. I will never leave this village, his mind repeated as he listened to the footsteps, listening so intently that every other sound was distilled, fading into the background of his hearing. The boy stood up.

The moon was completely hidden, and he could see nothing. The thought of the spider directly above him filled him again with terror. Thread-like fingers seemed to cling to his face, enmeshing it, but when he raised his hands to pull them away there was nothing.

Then he saw the moon uncovering itself luridly, and the cold light fell on a figure at the door. The boy took a step back.

The moon had fallen from the sky and stood now before him, white, strange, sighing, sad.

The moon, the moon, the boy's mind shouted.

Then he looked above him through the thatch, and the moon was still in the sky, had not fallen.

The fear was gone. Whoever was at the door could not fill him with the horror of the moon. He walked slowly toward the figure there.

It was the girl.

The boy breathed evenly now.

"I thought the moon had fallen," he said. "You were so white in the light."

The girl stood framed and still in the silver light of the moon.

"Move from the door," the boy said. He shuddered again at the sight of her against the light.

The girl came into the hut.

"It is very lonely here," the boy said softly. "And it is so very hot, too. Does it never rain here?" He longed for the sound of another voice. Until the girl spoke she would remain a ghostly apparition.

The girl did not answer for a long time, did not move yet. Still standing near the door, she said, "Yes, it rains. And soon it will be the season of the rain," and then she was silent, and then she resumed almost hesitantly, "Soon, but no one can tell when, not even the men who must fire the brush of the *milpas*."

She sat down near the boy, who was lying on the ground looking through the thatch into the sky.

The girl had spoken, and the moon was again only the moon. The boy said, "The sky is so black, so deep. So deep and black that it seems like the sea." He jumped up quickly like a child. "And so if I stand looking up," he laughed, "I will see myself reflected, as if I were looking down into the sea." He gazed into the sky, searching vainly. "Have you ever seen the sea?" he asked her.

"No," she answered, then hesitantly, "I have lived here always." Her eyes were fixed on her hands, her face turned guiltily toward her lap.

"The sea is peaceful and cool at night," the boy said. "I have been there many times," he said remembering.

His expression changed all at once, the intenseness of his features becoming subdued. There was a suggestion of tenderness in his voice, and he said, "The sea is peaceful, and I would stand on the shore letting the water wash my feet." He was holding the crucifix about his neck, his fingers caressing it tenderly.

"Do you want to hear the sea?" he asked her, smiling. He knelt before her, where she sat on the ground. He cupped his hands to her ear in imitation of a shell. "Can you hear it?" he asked her eagerly, still like a child excitedly.

She listened intently for a moment. "Is it the sea?" she asked incredulously.

"Yes," he answered smiling, still holding his cupped hands to her ear. "Everyone carries the sea in his hands." He paused for a long moment, the smile passing, "She . . . She used to tell me that," he said hurriedly. He dropped his hands from her ear, and immediately he reached for the wooden cross about his neck. He cupped it in his hands, like a boy with a precious possession. He was still kneeling near the girl.

She turned her face toward his. Their eyes met. She parted her lips, as if to whisper to him, but the unformed words seemed to choke, and the mouth closed.

He frowned. He felt the girl's eyes on his face as intensely as he had felt the accusing gaze of the moon. The fear which was now a coldness mingled with unbearable sadness, seized him again, and he said hurriedly, "I lived once near the sea. Very near." His voice disembodied, like that of a person speaking automatically to dispel an unpleasant memory. He looked up, seeking the spider, seeing, without noticing that it had finished its weaving and seemed now to be waiting for something.

The eyes of the girl were still on the boy's face.

Accusing, the boy thought, not daring to look at the girl, to meet the gaze again, repeating, "I lived near the sea, when I was just a child." He moved from the girl.

"When I was still with her . . . " he said. Then he stopped abruptly, his hands clung to the crucifix with more intensity, his fingers touching the tiny wooden face, the crucified arms, feeling them tenderly. "When I was still with her," he repeated silently, as if that was all that he had heard of what he had spoken.

Then the tense gaze that the boy had felt so acutely relaxed. The girl turned her face guiltily away once again. Her hand rested within the folds of her skirt.

"When I lived by the sea," the boy went on hurriedly, but more deliberately, "we lived in a magnificent house." And he was remembering the many times that he sat surrounded by the poor men and women who had listened to his child's voice spinning out the stories of golden palaces.

"Yes," he said, almost to himself. "It was like a palace, that house where we lived when I was a child, when . . . " He faced her, knowing that her accusing gaze was no longer on him. "Do you know what a palace is?" he asked, and before she could turn to face him, he looked away, at the waiting spider that fascinated him, so removed from him and the girl.

"No," the girl sighed.

The boy stood over her. His eyes were wide, like long ago, and now they were demanding, yes, but differently demanding, like a very young child, innocently.

"It was bright and dazzling, in that palace where we lived," he said. He closed his eyes. The image filled his mind. "And the steps were . . . " He opened his eyes, looking at the girl, challenging her to doubt, "mirrors," he almost shouted. "The windows reached to the sky itself, and the floor, the floor was glass, brilliant, and we danced together so long ago," he said, softly, to himself, "so very long ago, when I was still a child." He released the crucifix, but still he watched it lying there on his chest, saw the tiny head, the nailed hands, so small but so clear, so real. He looked at the girl, not challenging this time, but imploring her to believe.

Her eyes rose slowly, and they fell on the cross, the tiny wooden cross that he embraced so urgently. Then again her eyes met the boy's. Again her eyes accused. Again her lips parted, and the words seemed to be about to form. But again the lips closed, the words remained unspoken, her eyes fell to her lap, studying her hands in the folds of her skirt.

"We would dance all night, she and I," he said, loudly and very, very hurriedly. He covered his face, uttering a sound like a gasp, then laughing nervously. "The music would be like the sea," he shouted, then more softly, listening intently as if to hear it again, "It would start softly. Softly," he said. His voice became harsh, and he raised his hands to his ears. "We would spin, and around and around and . . . " He turned to the girl, searching her face, no longer afraid of the gaze. "Do you believe me?" he pled. The urgency made his voice tremble.

"I believe you," the girl said, feeling the urgency, and the sadness, like her own, as she felt.

She stood up, very straight, thinking the unformed words furiously, knowing that she must form them now.

"Yes, I believe you," she repeated.

And she could see clearly the urgency in the pleading eyes, and she felt an affinity with this strange boy even more than the physical attraction, more, much more, and she stood very near him, looking deeply and without shame now into his eyes, and her heart seemed to burst, and her body almost touched his.

"Love me," she whispered.

The words echoed in his crowded mind. He frowned as if he did not understand. Then he recoiled from her like a wounded animal. The wooden crucifix spun about as he turned from her. As if he were afraid that it would leave him, he twisted it around, holding it tightly in his hand.

She stood against the door, where the light of the moon was silver and ghostly.

"I . . . " he started. He took one step toward her. He clenched the tiny cross, and seeing her again white like the moon, he covered his face, shouting, "Move," and when he uncovered his face again, his eyes sought the spider. *Reality*, he thought frantically, *reality.*

"Go away," he whispered to the girl. "Leave me alone."

And her voice filled the room again, piercing the darkness and the heat,

"Love me."

"I . . . " The perspiration made his clothes cling to his body.

He thought, *The cobwebs are enmeshing me.* And the spider seemed to be watching him, hiding also from the light of the moon.

"I love you," she whispered.

"Listen," he said, moving toward her, wanting desperately to stop her words, to forget them. "I am going to be a dancer. Do you want me to tell you?"

She opened her mouth to speak but he interrupted her frantically. "No," he said, "no, no . . . please. Please." He was almost begging. "Just listen."

Again, she opened her mouth, but he went on, drowning out her words. "I am going to be a dancer. Listen, and I will tell you." He whirled his body. "I will dance and dance," he continued hurriedly, fearing her words, fearing that she would speak. "No, listen. Like this. They will shout bravo, *qué magnífico*,[32] and they will all praise me, and love me."

He glared at the girl angrily, as if now she was a rival, and he whispered, "I will dance forever."

The girl's lips did not move this time, did not even try to form the words.

"And they will write about me," the urgent voice said, "and my name everyone will know." He embraced himself, looking up at the cold stars as if he would read his name there, but he saw the moon in the black sky, and he turned away quickly. "And the big ones, they will call me by my name, but I will only nod to them, I will not smile, no, that would be too much, and they shall all give fiestas in my honor, and wait upon me always, and I shall never stop dancing, and they will all love me."

He whirled about, making a sound like laughter or a desperate moan, a gasp, a smothered sob.

"I shall dance forever and ever," he cried, "and never stop."

He paused, breathing harshly. And it was as if he had been transformed as he looked at the girl, his face gleaming with perspiration, his hair over his eyes, his mouth open. He twisted, whirled his lithe body, gasping.

"Pablo!" he cried out. "They will all shout my name—he is the greatest dancer of them all."

Passion flared into anger in the girl, and she lunged at him, scratching at his flesh.

"Don't," he shouted. He thrust his arm out and pushed her fiercely from him.

---

[32]How wonderful.

Exhausted, she leaned against the door and she was weeping like a lonely child.

He went to her, and he touched her face gently, which was streaked with tears. "Don't. I . . . " he started once more, now to himself, sadly, sadly. "I . . . I cannot . . . love you."

She turned her face to him, and his hands still held her face.

"Please . . . " he said, and his eyes and voice were undemanding. "When you cry," he said, "it is like . . . " He did not finish. Instead, he sighed with cold loneliness, no longer fear but isolation. And then he said, "Like in the palace with the mirror walls and the glass steps."

He removed his hands from her face, and he touched the crucifix about his neck. "Like in that house with the gleaming floors and the . . . " He moved under the place where the moon entered through the thatch, and the light pounced upon him accusingly. He recoiled from it, crying, "It's a lie, it's a lie. Everything. The palace and the mirrors and the glass steps."

She had stopped weeping now, feeling again the unbearable urgency of the boy.

"I was born in the filth," he said dully, standing now unafraid directly under the light of the moon. "Not in a palace but in the filth. At night we could hear the shouting. And the music . . . the music was the shouts of the drunk men coming home.

"But . . . " Again his voice was anxious. "But we did go to the glowing palaces. We did. Because she would sit with me holding me tight in her arms, because I was just a child, and I felt so secure, safe, as if . . . as if I had never been born, and she told me then of the palaces and . . . "

Now he was looking at the crucifix, speaking to it now. "And she would sing," he went on. "Softly. Until I was asleep, until I could no longer hear the shouting, the. . . . " He moved from the light. "In the dark," he whispered to himself, trance-like, "in the dark, it is easier." Then in a harsh voice, he said, "And then he would come, and he was my father."

He moved back farther into the dark. "And he hated her because she loved me, and he hated me more, and he shouted, and he was drunk, and he told me he would kill me when I slept, and I would be alone, and I lay awake not daring to sleep, waking up suddenly when at last I did fall asleep, running to her, watching to see that she was breathing, and then, the same day, he tried to kill me, and she knelt before him pleading, and he hit her. Then the blood . . . No," he said. "No."

On a silver string, the spider swung across the small hut. For a moment the boy could see its legs moving grotesquely. He stared fascinated, watching until it had disappeared.

Then, still watching the spider, he said, "She would tell me about the palaces in the city where we would live, some day. And she was so beautiful, and I loved her so much," he said, holding the cross. "And I was so afraid that something . . . that she . . . And then one day she was sick." He opened his mouth, but his hands covered the gasp. He sighed deeply, filling the room with the lonely sound. "And they came for her," he said. "And they took her away in a large black box. And I . . . I . . . I was left . . . alone. And the man never came back. And she was in that cold black box. And I . . . I was . . . alone."

He tore the crucifix from his neck and brought it desperately to his mouth. "Mother," he whimpered.

In the morning the boy woke with the rising of the sun, and his body was wet with perspiration. He had been dreaming in troubled sleep. Awake, now, he felt like a stranger in a hostile world. He looked about him, remembering the girl. Then he lay back on the ground, not daring to move because each movement brought more perspiration to soak his body.

He remembered the man the girl had said would help him reach the city. He sat up. The sunlight through the thatch fell on his face, bursting with a white shattering.

He walked out of the thatch hut and he could see that the village had awakened much earlier, for children were out in the distance and he heard the loud and clear ringing of a bell in the steamy air. There were no men, except the very, very old.

They have not returned from their fields, he thought. *Or if they have, they are gone again. She must take me to him,* he thought. *I must find her.*

But he was filled with anxiety at the thought of seeing her again. He did not have to look for her, because turning he saw her standing by the door of the house, and he could see behind her, inside, the woman kneeling before the heated stones making the food for breakfast. He walked toward the house, forgetting for a moment his urgent need of the man and remembering now only the hunger. He felt a wave of heat sweep over him, cold heat, not the heat of the sun, but something else from within, fragments from the frenzied night of yesterday.

The girl and the boy stood before each other as undecided as animals meeting in the jungle ready to fight or pass on silently. Then the heat was that of the sun only, no longer from within. The night past was yesterday, not the present.

"Where is the man?" the boy asked.

Except for the movement of her lips as she answered, the girl did not move. "He has not returned," she said, and she too was remembering the night past.

And now again her hair was tightly braided, and she was dressed as she had been yesterday, with the skirt and the blouse, when she had led him to this house. Only this time, there was a necklace of ruby-red beads about her neck.

The boy cast furtive glances at the woman inside. The wafting scent of food stirred his hunger.

The girl understood. She went to the woman. Without speaking, she got the small round flat kneaded maize and placed it over the heated stones, and she knelt there like the woman, and then she turned the tortilla until it was brown, until the odor was that of the cooked maize. Then she brought it in the palms of her hands and gave it to the boy.

When he had finished eating, he asked, "Will you take me to the man?" Again, he could not face her. The heat swelled like a tide from within. He looked toward the ground. "I must reach the city," he said as if to himself.

"Yes, she answered, "I will take you to him now."

She walked from the house, away from the woman without speaking, and he followed her, and she walked quite straight and with the dignity of the ancient people who had once long ago given themselves to the sun.

They passed the small house of the cross. A man sat there before the door sleeping, and when the girl passed, he woke, crossed himself, and chanted urgent words. Soon they had left behind them the thatch houses.

Now, the boy was walking beside the girl. A deer fleeted across their path, and for once the girl laughed, and when she turned to look at the boy, he was smiling.

As they proceeded still farther, their steps shortened, becoming slower.

"It is far from here," she said. "His *milpa* is farther from the village than those of the others," she said.

The sun was hotter now, but it was cooler here because they were walking through the shade of the trees, but the earth was scorched and the boy felt his feet burning, and he had to stop, touching the soles of the shoes which had holes in them, but the girl, who was barefooted, did not feel the heat.

"Wait," the boy said. He sat on the ground. "I have been walking so long," he said. "I am tired."

She sat down, not near him but in front of him.

A short distance away was the cross marking one of the four entrances to the village. Above it, hanging from a tree, was a small crude, faded doll. The rope was very thick and very old.

"It marks the entrance to the village," the girl said when she noticed the boy looking at the cross.

"But there," he said pointing. "Above the cross. See? Hanging from the tree. What is it?"

"It is the effigy of a saint," she answered. "But I do not know why it is there. It has been there very long, since before I can remember."

The boy laughed easily. "It is very strange."

"You are not of our people," the girl said, "and you cannot understand. You come from the city of the Mexican people."

"Yes," he answered. He closed his eyes, dreaming of the city, and his legs were propped before him, his arms resting on his knees. "Yes, from the great city." He sighed, opening his eyes, destroying the image. "It is so wondrous there," he said. "There are so many lights, along all the streets, you see, and there is music and dancing and singing."

She looked away from him, toward the saint-effigy hanging above the distant cross. She was feeling the distance between her and the boy.

"I . . . " she started hesitantly. "I have wanted often to go there . . . to that city."

"It is like a jewel," he said, and he had not heard her. "Like a sparkling jewel."

"These," she said, fingering the beads about her neck, "these are from that city. A man passed through here once," she said, "who sold them to my father for much money. And yet, once I had an amulet, which. . . . " She stopped. She extended the necklace to the boy. "See?"

But he was looking above at the watery sky.

She held the beads in her hand, leaning toward him so that he might take them.

But he had not been listening. He rose now.

"Come," he said, "we will never see that man if we wait longer."

The man saw the girl walking toward the field, and then, behind her, the boy. The man put his hand to his forehead to ward off the sun. *It is she,* he thought. *It is she, and someone is with her.*

And when he thought the last, he felt the perspiration cold, as if each droplet had solidified on his body into tiny pieces of unmelting ice. He took one step forward. Then he stopped. He stopped motionless there amid the felled brush drying in the now furiously cold-scorching sun, and he thought, without doubt, with only a fatal certainty, *She is going to leave me.*

The boy wiped the perspiration from his brow. Seeing the man now, he felt afraid and very lost. "Is that the man?" he asked, and with each word the perspiration flowed more copiously.

"Yes."

All three stood silently there for a long time, and each was thinking furiously, each as if all their life previously had been a prologue to this one moment, which strangely was not turbulent but silent, like a moment out of time suspended and waiting in space to be carried away soon into the vortex of memory, but always present, always now.

At last the man moved. He walked through the felled brush barefooted. His face was set and dark and harsh, and his eyebrows spoke of anger, and sadness, and that saddened anger coursed through every sinew of his body. His long dark hair shone fiercely under the light of the sun, and he looked like a jungle animal seeking prey.

Then he was facing the boy, trying not to look at the girl.

"You," the man said to the boy, "what do you want?"

Because the man spoke in the tongue of the ancient people, the boy could not understand. "I need help," the boy said in the words of the flourishing race, and looking at the man. He was thinking, *I will never return to the city.*

The girl was silent, looking at her father, but she stood near the boy.

The man tried desperately not to face her.

"You," the man said now in the language the boy knew, "what do you want?" He felt the void of loneliness. He was looking evenly at the boy, and he sensed, though he would not understand, the mystery and the franticness, and he thought too of the girl, his daughter, and he knew what would happen, and he wanted to kill this boy of the lithe body, to kill him and have time pass covering the act until the girl would forget, because the man had turned toward the girl and he had seen in that glance the love for the boy whom he hated, and he hated the girl too, in that moment, whom he loved, for wanting this boy, and his own need of the girl, his daughter, was very, very great.

The boy's eyebrows drew together and he said finally, sensing the hatred from the man, "I have been walking for many, many days. I am lost, I must find the village where the train will take me to the city. I need help." And he thought, *He will not help me. I will have to wander endlessly.*

Again the man stared harshly at the boy, hating. Still, the girl did not speak, hardly moved.

"I . . . cannot show you the way," the man said, hating very, very much, wanting to hurt this boy in any way.

"But if you do not help me . . . " the boy started. "Those other people turned from us, and they will not . . . "

"You will have to leave," the man said. "Alone. Alone, you will have to find your way."

"Please . . . " the boy pled.

"Look," the man shouted, motioning to the felled brush. "The rain has not come yet. But soon it will come. The brush must be burned before the rain," he said. "I cannot leave my *milpa*. For you."

"Please . . . " the boy started again, but the girl turned away, and he stopped speaking, turning to look at her for a moment, then at the man.

"Go," the man said. "Leave my *milpa*, leave this village. Now," he said.

"You will not help me," the boy said quietly.

"Leave," the man shouted.

Then the anger rose in the boy. The days under the sun, and the trees cutting, the heat and the stabbing weeds, the hunger and the thirst, the desperate hoping that perhaps in the next village he would find help—all passed swiftly through his mind, and his face was distorted horribly, and he reached swiftly for a stone on the ground, and like a tiger he lunged at the man with a moan.

But the man moved swiftly, and the stone hit his shoulder. The blood came red. The man touched his shoulder, bringing his hand before him, and he seemed ready to lunge at the boy, but as he moved forward, he saw the girl, his daughter, watching him, and the blood came, and again he wanted to kill the boy, but the face of the girl made him turn wordlessly, realizing, himself, that the dream of happiness was shattered.

The girl came to him then, touching the bleeding shoulder. And she looked into the man's eyes, and she felt the love for that man, but she felt also the necessity of what she must do, and she wiped the shoulder with her skirt and she tore that skirt and tied the cloth where the blood came. And she looked at the man wordlessly, very long.

He understood, and he turned from her, walking back to his *milpa*, seeing in the cold impassive sky the stone face of the god of long ago.

"I will take you to that village. I will help you find the city." The boy and the girl sat again resting there by the cross with the shadow of the saint-effigy falling before them like a hanged man.

The boy looked up quickly. "When?" he demanded.

"Tomorrow," she answered.

"Now," he said.

"It will be dark," she said, looking at the sky.

"Can you find it?" he asked urgently. "Are you certain?"

For a moment she did not answer. She looked away, again at the sky. "I am certain."

He stood up quickly. "Tomorrow," he whispered. Then he spun about, and his shadow whirled in the light of the sun, converging with the shadows of the trees, and he said, "Look, do you see my shadow?" And he whirled again laughing.

This time the girl was not looking at him, not listening. She was staring beyond, wondering, thinking, *Tomorrow.*

"This is the doll of good fortune," the boy was saying then. "Here, I will give it to you." He reached for the saint-effigy, pulling it from the tree where it hung. He held the faded doll in his hand, the rotting rope about its neck falling to the ground.

"No," the girl shouted when she saw him. "No," she whispered frightened.

"I am giving it to you," he laughed, and he extended the doll toward the girl.

She took it.

She touched it with care, and she looked at it intently, like a mother seeing for the first time the child to whom she has given life, but there was a look of horror on her face as she saw the tiny effigy, the crude-drawn almost completely faded lines of the face, the tiny clasped hands, the grotesquely small body.

The boy was still laughing. "It will bring you good fortune," he said joyously, "when you return to your village."

"No," the girl said, and she was still staring at the doll.

"I will not return to the village."

"You will not return to . . . ?"

"No," she said. "I am going with you. You will take me with you to the city."

Quietly, she knelt at the foot of the yellow-white cross, laying the doll there like an unwanted child.

5

"The world," said the old, old woman with the frozen eyes like tears, "is a very vast place."

She leaned on an old stick, and her hands one over the other were like the protruding roots of a dying ancient tree. Her voice was hardly audible, and it seemed to come not from her mouth but from her eyes, which were fixed, and her hair was white and silky like tangled cobwebs.

"And the corners of that world are far, far distant from each other. The land stretches mightily to the end of the sky, and there the sea touches it and flows on and on into eternity. And eternity . . . who can know eternity? It is the land and the sky and the sea and time, the past and the future, and even more, beyond comprehension, all fusing."

She straightened as much as she could, the silver webs on her hair trembling, and she raised her stick pointing to the sky. "You ask me to reach into that something called eternity, into the dark corner called future, which is only a small thing in infinity, but oh so great for those like you and me who are certain only of past, not even present, because that is less than a pinpoint becoming even now the past . . . for I can say to you, now, and when I have formed the word, which itself will have a beginning and end, that now will be gone, and a new one forming, all inevitable. Yet you ask me to reach into that something called future to help you find the boy whom you lost."

The girl looked into the colorless hypnotic eyes of the old woman, whose voice wheezed weirdly like wind through the thatch of an old house, and she saw in those eyes the meaning of the words she could not understand.

"Yes," the girl said. "Can you tell me? Will you tell me, old woman?" The girl spoke to the old woman of the boy whom she loved, and of the desperation in him and of the mystery and the strangeness, of how she would have gone with him to the city, and she told also of how the man, her father, was not in the village nor in his *milpa*, of how he had gone, she knew, to show the boy the way, knowing that she would have left him.

She would have continued, but the old woman shouted, "Why do you tell me this? Why do you come to me with your burden and your sadness and your share of pain?"

"Because I must find him," the girl said. "Because I will find the city and find him, if you . . . Because . . . "

"Yes," said the old voice, calm now. "I know. I know, and understand." The glazed eyes were unblinking and dead, and only the hair seemed alive. Now she stood over the small fire in the center of the room, and she rubbed the decayed roots that were her hands, because all warmth had left her body long ago, many, many years ago, and she was cold, freezing in the stifling heat.

"But you are so young," came the disembodied voice, "and I am so old, so very, very, very old, and so you cannot understand, you cannot know. You do not understand that others like you have come to me out of the black night with the wringing hands and the pleading eyes and the unbearable sorrow which becomes my own. Yes, many others like you have asked me for help. And once in the past which is only yesterday in eternity, a boy who was a man sat before me, and his child was dying in the village, and the holy men chanted to save his life, and I told him of the evil lonely spirit of the Pol who possessed his wife, and I spoke of the severed head and of the salt on the wound to ward away the evil, because I had looked into that thing called future and seen . . . "

She buried her stick into the dying fire, turning it until the flames seemed to sigh, to sigh and glow and come alive again.

"And that man believed but did not listen . . . so long ago, so many years, so many lives ago," she said, and her voice had risen, as if the warmth of the tiny flames was giving her strength. "And he fled into the night with the child, fled through the jungle like a lonely animal becoming fierce in isolation, and he died there in the jungle, I know, also like a desperate lost animal." She was trembling now with the cold from within, and she bent over, and her fading hands reached for the girl's, warming herself with the young one's warmth.

"And so you come to me," said the old fading voice. "And if I tell you, Do not search for the boy who is gone, for you will not find him, the hope will be dead and so too the life. And if I say, Search for him for you will find him, then I would perhaps know that you would not find him, and you would not know it, and you would search like all the lonely wanderers. But if I say nothing, if I do not reach into infinity, then you will not know, and you will hope, and you will live that life of hope, the hope which relies on coincidence, the coincidence which is life, the life which is not of three dimensions, which is infinitesimally greater and excludes no possibility."

The girl looked into the fire. The woman had released her hands, and now the girl knelt on the ground with her hands on her lap.

She said quietly, "Yet if you looked into what you call future and saw that I would find him, then . . . "

"No," wheezed the old woman, with whatever of passion was left in her. "I must not do it. Let the future slide down the mountain of present into the pit of past, and then you will know."

"But why will you not tell me, old woman?" the girl pled. She still gazed into the expiring fire, because the face of the old woman was a horrible maze of wrinkles.

Now the fire had begun to die, and smoke was rising, very straight in the unmoving air, and the old woman bent for a stick, casting it into the fire. The fire rose in a moment, and in another moment the stick was embraced by the consuming flames.

"Look," said the old woman, pointing into the fire. "That stick was lying on the ground, and I have picked it up and thrust it into the fire, and soon it will be nothing. Do you see the flames piercing it? Listen. Do you hear the sound as it burns? Do you hear it weeping with pain?"

"Yes," the girl said.

The stick broke and became two, and now it was black, and it was no longer moaning, now sighing, dying.

"And if the tree had known," said the old, old woman, "that its branches would burn up in fire, would it have dared to grow? Now do you understand?" she said, a worn note of pity in her voice. "Do you see why I will no longer reach into the corner of eternity named future?"

Now the girl looked up, her face without expression. "I am not afraid of the secret knowledge," she said, then pleaded, "Oh, tell me, old woman, tell me if I will find him, tell me if I will find that boy whom I love,"

Again the woman sighed, as the dead twig now ashes had done. She bent over once more placing more sticks in the fire, and she stood over the small flames, peering with the colorless, glazed eyes into the pit of the still-glowing ashes. "Oh, foolish girl," said the old woman, without anger, with something like sorrow, and her eyes were softened by the fire. "I have spoken to you of these things of the sea and of the future and of eternity and the night. I have talked of tragedy and of death, and still you do not understand. Still you would know. But it is useless," she sighed. "Go," said the voice now, without harshness or anger, with only the same weariness and sadness as before. "Leave me quickly. Why must you come to me adding to my sorrow? I who have looked for others where you would have me search, I who have always seen . . . " She looked up quickly from the fire. "Go," she shouted.

The girl rose. "Then I will go to the city," she said, not to the woman but to herself now, and once the words were formed, there was also the determination. "And I will find my way," she said, and she knew that she would go, and she knew with certainty that she would some day find the boy of the longing desperate yearning eyes, and that he would love her then as she loved him. "I will find him," she said.

The old woman stared after the girl, after the dimming mist, which was all the old woman's eyes were capable of seeing now.

Then the girl disappeared into the trees.

The old woman returned to the fire. The glazed eyes were weeping, although no tears came.

"Oh, foolish girl," she wept, "I have spoken to you of the future and death and of the night and eternity, and still you do not understand."

The fire died, and the tiny pit at the foot of the old, old woman was smothered with ashes.

PRESENT: The City

"But eventually the night claims all her sordid children, and her shroud is soothing, and the sleep is quiet and endless."

SIX: The Night

1

In the room next to hers in the dilapidated hotel that smelled of decadence lived a man and his wife, and they had five children, and the man and the woman watched the girl sadly, sensing the dark mystery, and they watched her come in nightly. They saw too the young man who lived with her, the sad lonely young man of the sensitive lonely face.

They saw them there every day, and in the morning the young man would leave, and the girl would remain in the room. Often the young man would not return until very, very late, when the girl had left already, and she would leave very often in the night, alone, returning many hours later, alone.

Then the man and woman of the five children next door would hear the voices, never loud, subdued except sometimes, and the young man would speak softly for very, very long. He did not speak in the language of the Mexican, nor in the Indian of the girl, but he spoke in another tongue, which the man and the woman listening intently and unmoving could not understand. But they did understand the franticness of the young man and the very young girl, and they knew that the words, though soft and subdued, were agonized and anxious.

And they wondered.

Then one day the woman spoke to the girl, when the girl was alone, when the young man had left early. "You are very lonely, *chica*," said the woman. "I can see it. You are sad, too, like the young man who lives with you. What makes you so sad, *chica*, what is it you long for? *Chica*, have you lost a mother? Has your husband lost a mother?"

"He is not my husband," the girl said

"Oh," said the woman, and she sighed sadly.

They were standing both in the narrow hall. Although it was morning, it was very dark in the corridor, and the sun came in only through a small window at the opposite end from where they stood, and where the light came in, it seemed to enter reluctantly, screened by the filthy glass.

"I see," said the woman now, without surprise because she had known it somehow. "Listen, *chica*," she said, "come into my room. The children are outside, and two others are asleep. So we can talk, *chica*. Because you seem very lonely. And I would like to help you so much. If you will only let me, *chica*."

She placed her hand gently on the girl's shoulder, and she led her into the room where she, the mother of the five children, lived with her husband.

Inside, it was very close and narrow, and there were only two rooms, and in this room where they stood now was an old bed. It was made of metal and was very ornate and quite old. The room was incredibly ugly and crowded, like all the others in this hotel, with mattresses lying on the floor. But it was also immaculately clean, this room, and serene, unlike that of the girl.

Against the wall was a small bed, where two children slept, one larger than the other, both huddled together.

The woman sat on the bed. She held the girl's hand.

"Is he cruel, that young man?" she asked. "Is that why you are so sad, so lonely? Tell me, *chica*. I would like so very much to help you." The woman's face was contorted, and she felt the genuine pity and the love for this girl. She wanted very much to help her. Not curiosity, but an affinity to sadness itself, led her to question.

"No," said the girl. Her face was more slender now than it had been before, and her eyes seemed deeper now and more longing, more depthless now, and she was even more beautiful with the serenity of near-resignation on her face. "He is kind, very kind, and he helps me very much."

The woman sighed. "You are a strange girl, *chica*," she said, "and you are so beautiful and so mysterious, and I watch you go out at night and return alone to that young man, and you are so lonely and so sad. Why, *chica?*" She placed her hand again on the girl's shoulder. She repeated, "Have you lost a mother, *chica?*"

"No," said the girl, and then she said, very softly and without emotion, "Once, in a village where I was born, a boy passed, and I loved him very much, and I would have gone away with him, but my father felt it and he showed the boy the road he searched for. And I have come to the city to find him."

"But the young man," the woman said, "what of him with whom you live? Does he know, *chica?* Do you love him?"

"No. I do not love him," the girl said. "And I think he knows of the boy. I have told him, but he does not understand my language, and I think he knows. I am sure he feels. Yes, he knows."

"Oh, *chica*," said the woman, rising from the bed and clenching her hands. "How long have you been searching for this boy?"

"Since I have come from the jungle," the girl answered. "Since I was brought here by the holy man who helped me when I was sick and who showed me the way to the city."

The woman thought, *She has lived here only a few days, and so she has just come from the village of which she speaks.*

"And you have not found him, that boy? You do not know where he is?"

"I have not found him yet, "the girl answered, "but I will find him. Every night I . . . "

"Oh," the woman cried, and she wanted to clutch in her arms this very young girl and shelter her. "This is a port city, *chica*," she said. "And boats come and go daily, and people leave, never returning perhaps, and the boy you speak of, he may be gone, this city is not large, you would have found him. Oh, *chica*, perhaps he has gone to the capital city, away from this state. There are so many cities, the world is so very large, *chica*. How will you find him? How can you be sure?"

"No," the girl said, turning harshly on the woman. "You are wrong. You do not understand. He was coming to the city, and this is the city, and he is here, and I will find him, soon."

The woman stood over the girl, trying to understand. *She has come from the village,* the woman thought, *and she is only a child, so very young, perhaps sixteen, but one day she will understand what I have told her, when she is older, and then . . . and then . . . But now she does not know, and so she can hope, and why should I shatter that dream which will be shattered eventually, why should I destroy her hope, why should I kill her now?*

"Yes," the woman said with conviction, sensing more than ever the secret dignity of the girl. "Yes, you will find him, *chica*," she said. "Some day." Now she walked across the room, and she stood with her back to the girl.

And the girl went to the woman.

And she said, "Can you help me?"

The woman faced her.

"Yes," she said.

She turned her back again, away from the girl. "See," said the woman, pointing to a small niche in the wall.

Inside the niche was a small statue of a woman, and the woman there was dressed completely in black and she was hold-ing her hands clenched to her breast as if in the wordless agony of desperation. At the foot of the statue was a crude candle burning in a red glass.

"It is beautiful," the girl said, staring into the face of the statue. And she remembered the statue that she had held once and broken in the house-of-the-cross. And she remembered the face on the amulet of long ago.

"Do you know what it is?" said the woman.

"It is a saint," the girl answered.

"It is the mother of sorrows," the woman explained. "Do you see the anguished face? She has known sorrow, too, and pain, like you perhaps, only greater."

"She is beautiful," the girl said. The light from the candle had begun to flicker, and the niche grew darker and darker and the virgin of sorrows seemed to become alive.

"Look at the face," said the woman. "It is very anguished." She reached for another candle on a table beside the niche, and she lighted it from the other and placed it in the red glass. "It must never go out," she said. Then she said to the girl, "Do you know what prayer is, *chica*?"

"Yes," the girl answered.

"And can you pray, *chica*?"

"No," the girl said. "I have never prayed."

"Ah, then, *chica*, you must," the woman said. "You do not have to believe," she said, "but you must pray. Here," she said, "take it, *chica*. I will give it to you, if you want it, and I would like very much for you to have it, *chica*. It will help the loneliness." She reached into the niche and brought forth the virgin of sorrows.

The girl took it from the woman. She studied it, seeing the pale face, the sorrowful eyes.

"Ask her for help," said the woman. "And leave the candle burning always. You do not have to believe. But you must pray," she said. "Ask her to let you find the boy you seek. And the peace," she said. "You do not have to believe," the woman said, "you do not have to believe."

She walked in the night through the deep-black shadows, across the city to the same places she had gone to over and over.

When she heard the music, she remembered the words of the boy, remembered with aching and longing, yearning, the desperate eyes. She would enter that place where the music was. The people would be dancing, and her eyes would search the faces, and the boy would not be there. The women there saw her, envying her youth and her beauty, and the sailors called to her, but she would walk away again through the city that never slept.

She walked endlessly thinking of many things, of the boy and of her love for him, of how he too must love her now, thinking of the lonely statue now in her room, of the man left behind in the village, of the silent woman, of the young man with whom she lived in the dilapidated hotel that smelt of decadence, and of him, that young man with whom she lived, she thought, *He is searching too, and I cannot know for what. He speaks to me, but I do not understand. And I cannot help him. Yet he too is desperate, I know. So strange and sad and lonely.*

On such a night as this she had met him, there at the docks toward which she was now walking, and in the deep shadows of the moonless night she had thought of the boy for whom she searched, and she thought, *I have found him, now he will take me, my body and soul, and I will have to search no longer.*

She had stood looking at him, at the dark shadow against the water, looking down as if lured by the peace of the sea. And then he saw her and moved from her, and she went to him, and then he came toward her also, silently. And they walked together then through the lonely night, still silently. Then they entered the hotel room where next to them the man and his wife lived with the five children.

It is not him, the girl had thought then, inside the room with the yellow light burning accusingly in the middle of the room. *It is not the boy I search.*

But she remained with this young man, who reminded her of the other because of the desperation. He did not speak her language, but the bond grew between them as they remained together, and he left in the mornings to go she knew to the docks, and he would return later. But he was not demanding. She left him almost nightly, and he would lie in the bed staring fixedly at the cobwebbed ceiling, at the yellow light bulb burning feebly in the center of the room.

And when she returned to him, he would take her with an urgency that was not desire, clutching her feverishly, his body fusing desperately, not passionately, with hers.

Afterwards he would lie on the bed sobbing sadly like a child in the night, and she would touch his face, remembering the boy whom she loved. Then the dark smile would come to her face, and she would think, *I will find him, some day, and then he will take me, my body and my soul, and I will no longer have to search in the night.*

Now again she had reached the docks where she had met the young man with whom she lived.

Now she stood watching the slow-shifting water, stood there as far away from the ships as possible.

Deep down in the deep-black water, the moon was drowning. The girl could hear its sad lonely weeping. The stars were bright and fierce and buried in the earth under the deep water. The girl stood looking down, thinking. Once she pushed a stone with her foot. The water shifted, dancing. She thought of the boy, of how once he had held his hands to her ear so that she would hear the sea. She sighed, the hope returned as it did always. This was the city, the only one she knew of and that was for her the world, and the boy must be somewhere, some place waiting for her, and so she would find him, some day.

The water settled, and the moon appeared again sighing. The clouds were reflected so misty and gray, deep down, that it seemed to the girl that the earth had been inverted, that the clouds were the shifting sea and the deep-blackness-sea was the sky. *And I am standing below looking up, not down,* she thought. *And so I must search for the boy not only along the streets, but in the deep dark places of the sea, which is the sky.*

A light flickered near her.

Turning, she saw a man standing a few feet from her. He had lighted a cigarette. He threw the match into the sea. The light died, sliding into memory, the sea. The girl walked toward the man. She felt again the excitement, the expectancy she felt when she thought, *It will be him.*

But she looked into his face, and it was not him.

Sighing, she walked away.

The man came to her now. She could see his image beside her as she looked into the watery sky. Then there were other footsteps. The man turned away, whistling. The sound of the whistling plunged into the water in search of the mournful wailing of the drowning moon. Then, only the mourning remained, the whistling had faded, where the light of the match had faded previously.

Now an older man stood next to the girl. The moon's reflection on his face revealed a crumpled shattered face.

"The sea is deep," said the man of the crumpled shattered face. "So peaceful, so quiet. Can you hear it sighing? Is it weeping?"

"It is not the sea," the girl said. "It is the moon. The moon is weeping."

The man looked into the girl's face. "Yes," he said. "Is the moon lonely? Is it weeping with loneliness?

"Yes," the girl answered, remembering her father in the *milpa* those long nights ago. "She is lonely because she cannot find the sun, her lover."

"Ah," said the man of the crumpling tired face, "the moon in search of the sun." He laughed mirthlessly, tragically. "It is a difficult search," he sighed.

"Look," the girl said to the man. "Look deep into the darkness of the sea."

The man moved closer to the water.

"Do you see the cloth which she is weaving?" she asked, pointing down at the reflection of the clouds covering the moon like a delicate white veil.

"Yes," the man answered.

"It is a hammock for her wedding night, when she will marry the sun," the girl said. "The hammock will not be finished until her search has ended."

The man no longer looked into the water.

"And when will that be?" he asked, looking at the girl. "When will the search end?"

The girl did not answer.

The man stared at her. "You look like the moon," he said. "You are so beautiful, so sad. So . . . young." The last word choked in his mouth. "Like someone I knew . . . strangely like him, somehow . . . a boy, a boy who . . . " Then quickly he said, "And do you search the sun too? And why? Why if you will never find him."

"Yet my father told me once," the girl said quickly, "that perhaps one day half the sky will be light and half will be dark, and the sun and the moon shall fuse, and the hammock will have been finished."

"No," the man said, "I do not believe the moon will ever find her lover."

"But perhaps . . . " the girl started urgently.

"Because," the man continued, "once they must have met, once, beyond time, once when the moon saw him and loved him. Once the sun must have seen the moon. But he . . . does the sun search for the moon?"

The girl said, "They met before the world was formed, long ago in the morning of time, and the moon saw the sun dancing. . . . " She stopped abruptly. "No, no . . . shining very golden. And sometimes in the morning after the sun has risen, the moon is like a faint ghost in the sky, and she sees him again, and that is perhaps her only happiness, seeing the evasive lover while she weaves her wedding hammock endlessly through the lonely night."

"And I . . . " said the man looking deadly white, "my search is as futile as the moon's. I have searched in the night too, hoping foolishly for the perfect union from young man to young man buying affection. But I will never find what I search for. Not my own youth, gone, lost in time, not that perfect union, not the young man lost in the past."

He looked at the girl intently, and sighed. "Yes," he said, "you look like him somehow, very strangely, infinitely young, infinitely secret. Young." He paused for a timeless time. "But eventually the night claims all her sordid children," he said, "and her shroud is soothing, and the sleep is quiet, and endless."

The man walked away.

The girl remained staring at the moon drowning in the deep black sea.

2

The mother of sorrows, which the woman with the five children had given the girl, rested on the small bare table opposite the bed. The candle in the red glass at the foot of the statue threw its pale yellow light on the plastic face, and the face was anguished and very, very real. The small pale supplicating hands of the virgin seemed occasionally to clench in the shifting light of the candle, and the lips seemed to move in unendurable pain, the eyes to turn agonizingly toward the cobwebbed ceiling.

Except for the candle, the room was in darkness. The yellow light bulb was turned off, and the lights from outside did not enter this side of the hotel. Heat hovered about the room heavily like the odor of a narcotic. Occasionally music from a strumming guitar penetrated the walls, coming from somewhere down the dark narrow corridor, monotonously slowly, very lugubriously, like a requiem.

The young man lay on the bed staring at the ceiling. There, the feeble light from the candle transformed thin cobwebs into knotted cords.

A few feet away, the girl knelt before the mother of sorrows, as the woman next door had taught her to do. In her hands, she held the mysterious rosary of that same woman, holding it only, not praying because she did not know the prayers, but asking over and over, as the woman had told her.

You do not have to believe, but ask. Ask, the woman had said, and that is prayer, the asking, and burn a candle always, and never let it die, because if it dies, that is hope extinguished, hope dead.

And so the girl lighted the candles and knelt before the mother of sorrows daily, not praying but asking, kneeling with the rosary held in her hands, facing the plastic face of the anguished statue.

Now the young man rose from the bed.

His face was pale in the yellow darkness of the room. His eyes looked browner, darker, almost black in the shadows. His eyebrows were thick, the hair dark, the eyes desperate.

He walked where the girl knelt, and he stood over her.

The stifling heat enveloped them in the close narrow room, and the music from the guitar was louder now and more doleful in its false happiness. The undershirt which the young man wore now clung to his body, his face gleaming in the yellow light. He looked intently at the statue before which the girl prayed.

"But don't you understand," he said softly, although he knew she did not know his language, "there is no god for the damned."

He sighed, looking sadly at the kneeling girl.

The girl rose from her knees. She was nothing more than a shadow with her back turned to the flickering candle.

"I have prayed for the boy," she said simply. "You do not understand my language, but perhaps you can feel what I say." And then she said, "And I have prayed for you."

He wiped the perspiration from his forehead, merely because the drops accumulating there glistened on his eyelashes and he felt dizzy, spinning.

"What is it you pray for?" he asked, forming the words slowly and deliberately, as if then she could understand. "What is it you long for so much that you search in the night, that you kneel there so often before the statue of the anguished face?"

"And you are so lonely," she said. She was sitting on the hard bed. In her hands she still held the rosary with the black tears. "You too are a wanderer. If you could speak my language, if I could understand your words, I would ask about your sadness.

I would tell you of the peace of which the woman of the five children has told me." Then she extended the rosary to him, wordlessly. She held it from the cross, and the beads fell grotesquely like a knotted rope.

"No," he shouted. He covered his face, recoiling from the girl. "Again and again," he said. "In the ceiling," he said, looking up where the tiny cobwebs were enlarged by the flickering candle flame. "Now the rosary too. Oh, god."

"What is it you hate?" said the girl. "What is it you fear? Why did you shout like that? Why do you turn away from the rosary? What is your loneliness? What do you hide from?"

She went to him and she placed her hand on his shoulder. He stood with his back to her. Again his hands were covering his eyes.

"If you could only understand," he said. "Oh, god, if I could tell you and have you understand, and you, you too, could speak, and from the two sorrows . . . "

"Once in a village a boy passed," the girl said, speaking only because she had to, because if he did not understand the words, he could still feel, could feel what she felt, and then the loneliness would be shared, the pain lightened, the hope growing, no longer isolated, so very, very, very alone. "And I loved him and I was going to go away from the village with him to the city, but my father understood, and he showed the boy the way to the city, and the boy did not return, and so I must find him, and he must find me, when he is a great dancer. In the night perhaps . . . "

The guitar had stopped playing, and now in the room there was another noise, a slow gnawing sound, like teeth biting on wood. The young man searched about frantically. In a corner of the room, a wrinkled mouse fed on a piece of bread. It turned its horrible tiny face toward the young man, and it was like a wrinkled old man, that mouse, or like a new-born child.

The young man turned away urgently with a smothered groan. "Like that face of long ago," he said, his hands pushing back the hair which had fallen over his forehead and rested oppressively there with the perspiration. "If I could tell you . . . " he repeated urgently to the girl, then more softly, "but then you would know the words and not understand, perhaps, not feel. But perhaps without knowing, feeling only, you could understand. Perhaps . . . "

The mouse had fled into a hole in the tracked wall through which the rotting wood-frame was visible.

The bread, a tiny crumb, remained there in the dark corner.

The girl sat looking at her hands, listening to the words, not knowing the words—feeling.

"Do you want to know why I am here?" he said. "Yes, let me tell you . . . you who do not understand, who cannot accuse, you who will feel."

"I cannot see the moon from here," the girl sighed. "Has it begun its search tonight, or is it resting? Is it tired? Can you see the moon? Has it begun its journey?"

"This is why," the young man said. "Because in another country, in my world, when I was still a boy, very young, when I was in school to be a doctor, divorced then from reality-life . . . " He stared at the face of the virgin of sorrows. Then he turned to face the girl. "Do you understand what I have been saying?" he pled. "Can you feel? Do you know, with your heart?"

The intensity of his voice made her move away from him, feeling very sad for him, wanting somehow to comfort him. She nodded, yes, she understood, she felt.

"The black night," he said. "Encased in it, all of us, you and me, together with your secret, your mystery, encased with mine too."

He was walking across the room, standing before the flickering candle in the red glass, returning then to the girl, looking finally into the crack where the mouse had disappeared, standing, often unmoving, listening for the sounds that did not come, for voices of the past long buried, lost in time.

"The man at the docks said the night will shelter all her children," said the girl. "Do you think that is true? Do you think there is escape?"

"I was to be a doctor," he said. "And all the hopes, the assurance, the belief . . . the light in the darkness. Then . . . and then do you know what happened? Will you listen if I tell you? Will you understand, with your heart? Do you know how I was introduced to . . . reality?"

"You are speaking of your sadness," said the girl. "But you are not alone," she said, feeling. "I know that sadness too, and the man at the docks . . . and there . . . see? . . . the sad mother of all sorrows. She is lonely too. Oh, she is clenching her hands. Do you see? Oh, will she never, never stop? Will the sadness never end?"

The guitar music commenced again, again slowly. Down the corridor, a woman screamed, a bottle crashed, a glass shattered, a child began to wail. The guitar strummed louder.

"The sound of life," he whispered to the girl. "Can you hear the dreadful shattering, crashing, wailing, screaming—the music of life? That is reality." He leaned closer to the girl. "Reality," he repeated. "But then, at that age, I had only heard of its existence, never really knew it, until that night—oh, god—will you listen if I tell you?"

"If you would take the rosary and ask," the girl said. "You do not have to believe."

"This is what happened that night," he said, hurriedly, as if speaking something that had never before been spoken. "I was in that room, and there was a knock, and it was a room so different from . . . this . . . so clean, and there were books and . . . and so clean . . . and lights . . . not darkness, not the sordid nar-

cotic heat, not the cobwebs, not the accusing yellow light, so feeble and weak and sad . . . so . . . human."

The child down the hall wailed louder, and the sound
entered the room from the dark silent narrow corridor like a
frightened echo.

"The child is crying," the girl said. "Because it must be fed.
I wonder if the doll at the foot of the cross in the village is a
child, too, weeping for food and the warmth to shelter it. I wonder if I killed it. I wish it would stop crying," she said.

"And I opened the door," the young man continued, and a
man stood there, but it was not a man, but reality. Do you
understand? Do you feel the words? And I opened the door.
Hurry, he said. Urgent, he said. Desperate, he said. Quickly, he
said. So I hurried out of the room . . . leaving behind me . . .
although how could I know it then? How? . . . All that was clean,
and we rode in that car, swiftly . . . the car speeding to my own
destruction, and I . . . and I . . . "

"Soon the flame will go out," the girl said, looking at the
candle. "And I must light another. The hope must not die."

The young man continued, "Desperate, urgent, quickly,
hurry, the man said. You must help me. He said, I cannot get a
doctor, you are a student, you can help me, it is too secret, I cannot get a doctor. He said, I am desperate, urgent, quickly,
hurry."

The gnawing sound began again, and the young man
listened. Then it stopped. The piece of bread was gone completely.

The young man continued, perspiring with each word,
breathing the heat. "Up the dark narrow steps, rushing. The
man was behind me. Where is the woman? I asked, and I was
responding to that instinct of one man to help another, and he
told me that I could help him, had to help him, that the woman
would die in labor, and so I must help him. Do you under-

stand?" he asked the girl. "But I didn't know," he went on hurriedly. "I didn't know until . . . "

"Now the weeping child has stopped," the girl said. She buried her head in her hands. Her face was streaked with tears. For a moment she was like the statue.

"No," he said. "Listen. I am telling you what happened." He sat down on the bed beside her. "When I got to the room, which was dark, I saw the woman lying on the bed, twisting in labor as the man had said. She was in labor, painfully, I thought. And the man who had brought me stood against the door looking at the woman on the bed, and she was groaning with pain, and I did not notice until very much later that her face was strange, so . . . so . . . yes, grotesque, weird, though soft, and very strangely child-like, as if a very small girl had painted herself. She was painted heavily, and her hair was bleached, but I wasn't noticing that then. I only knew that I had to help her quickly. She was twisting with pain, crying. She was groaning. I can hear it still." He stopped, as if listening for the sound to fade.

"In a moment the light of the candle will go out," the girl said. "Do you prefer the darkness?"

The young man was saying, "The labor had begun. The woman was twisting on the bed groaning. And then . . . and then . . . oh, god . . . " He covered his ears, as if again the horrible groaning had resumed.

The girl listened intently. *And you are speaking of your sadness* she thought, *and I understand. Yes, although I do not know. And I can feel.*

"Then . . . ," the young man stuttered. His body seemed to be in flame now, and he was soaked in perspiration. His breathing was harsh, like panting. "Then, when I touched the woman, when I was ready to—oh, god—I saw . . . that something was wrapped around her waist, and I turned it, the cloth there, unwinding it, unwinding the cloth around her body, about her waist, and then I knew . . . I saw . . . that this . . . person . . . who I thought was in labor . . . was not pregnant . . . was not even a woman . . . and I knew it was a man, and I kept unwinding the horrible thing, which was a bandage, or a cloth, a sash, unwinding it with a strange excitement now, something frightening, as if it was . . . " He was before the girl now, speaking urgently, demanding that she understand. "And when I had finished, I saw a small bundle pressed against this . . . man's stomach."

"You are sick with the loneliness," the girl said, "you are sick with pity. But look, now the moon is out, I can see its light faintly. Will it find the sun tonight?"

"It was a doll," the young man said. "It was a tiny, grotesque little carnival doll, and the man had tied it to his stomach. And the doll . . . the doll had feathers, pink and blue. And it was smiling . . . smiling . . . with all the feathers, with the golden-painted hair, with the terrible frightening pink celluloid doll skin. A doll, not a child. And the woman . . . was a man." He stopped abruptly. The silence thundered.

The girl rose from the bed. The rosary fell to the floor. The girl stood before the virgin of sorrows, watching the light, which was flickering.

"Then," the young man went on slowly, deliberately, "the man on the bed reached for the doll-child, he clutched it—tenderly, with love—to his breast, as if to feed it there, and with a sigh like the sigh of a woman ending the pain of labor, he . . . fainted . . . and the doll, the doll-child rested there like a dead baby."

"Mother of sorrows," the girl was whispering, "mother of sorrows, help him, help him too."

"After that," the young man went on dully, "I left the school, I had to. I couldn't think, couldn't read anything. And I walked through the dark streets. Like you, and I did not know what I searched for and wandered endlessly. Why? I asked myself. Why must I wander? What am I fleeing? That man cannot touch me. Yet . . . somehow, standing over the man . . . looking into the hideous painted face . . . I had seen . . . I had seen . . . and the excitement in me was . . . " He gasped, as if he could not finish, as if the unformed words must never be formed.

The girl came to him. She sat wordlessly beside him, listening intently, understanding.

"I did not return home," he went on. "I could not go back to what was clean. But I went to the large cities still searching . . . for what? I didn't know, and then, one day, I realized. . . . And then I knew my fate, which had been written on the face of that painted man of long ago, and still I fled farther, farther away, even to other countries . . . because," he said, shaking his head dazedly, "standing over that man of the child-doll, looking into the painted face, I had seen . . . I had seen . . . myself." He covered his face with his hands. "And the fear drove me here, to the docks where the water was peaceful, luring, where one night you came . . . you who can help me," he said, holding the girl urgently, "you who can keep me from sinking, from the dreadful unspeakable fear . . . springing upon me like . . . like this intolerable narcotic heat."

"Yes," the girl whispered, "yes."

He searched her face for a long time. The silence descended upon them heavily. Then he embraced her hard, tightly. He kissed her face desperately, her neck. Gasping, he lifted her in his arms and placed her urgently on the bed.

The candle flickered, sputtered.

Before his body came down on hers, he saw the rosary lying on the floor like a waiting noose, and with a gasp he moaned.

The light from the candle flickered one last time, and died.

When the girl returned from the streets the next night searching for the boy, she found the young man hanging with a noose about his neck. She made no sound, uttered no cry. She untied the rope. The body fell to her feet, and she knelt over it, pushing the young man's hair from his forehead, tenderly. Then she went into the hall and called the woman of the five children.

The woman came into the room, and she screamed. She touched the young man's face, which was cold and lifeless. She held his hands shaking them, desperately trying to force the life to return to the body. Tears filled her eyes.

"He was so sad" the woman said, rising resignedly from the floor. "So sad and lonely, and so young."

The girl was kneeling now before the statue of the mother of sorrows. She held the black-teared rosary in her hand.

Now you are alone again, the woman thought, standing over the girl. *But there will be others like this young man. And still you will search and search through the deep, labyrinthine night for the secret mysterious boy. And still you will not find him. What will become of you?* The woman thought, *When will the search end?*

The girl rose from her knees. Silently, she lighted the candle again.

The cheeks of the virgin were streaked with tears, and the girl stood staring into the weeping face.

SEVEN: The Mirror

I

Smoke filled the room in oppressive waves, now like a hand, reaching slowly across the lonely tables, over the shadowy night people, now like a shroud, lonely and sad—sad, and lonely like the discordant moaning notes coming from a trumpet.

And the savage relentless yellow light from the small improvised balcony pierced the smoke.

And in the center of the garish light, the boy danced.

About the room, listening now not even to the music, the sleepy tired over-painted women lolled thickly, hearing the obscene, vulgar, lurid comments of the lurid, vulgar men that reached for them with clammy fingers.

Against the walls, the waiters stood, no longer like vultures now, standing against the walls watching, seeing the lonely drunken men trying to capture what was never to be found, seeing the nervous painted young men glancing furtively toward the bar then with longing eyes toward the dancing boy, and seeing, those waiters, the boy himself dancing in the center of the light like a helpless worm writhing desperately in its last struggle for life beneath the sun-distilling magnifying glass of a wanton child, seeing all the harshness and the sadness, feeling the isolation of all these separate lives, seeing all this and not caring.

And the boy whirled, twisting the lithe, supple young body, moving his hands in slow sensual movements, making of the grating moaning music an exotic symphony of his own desperation.

And the music, vulgar, an imitation of a bolero, became louder and louder as the movements of the boy became more frenzied, passionate, desperate . . . until at last the music stopped, the music, the laughter, the sighs, the murmur of voices all bursting into silence. The light sent the smoke and the darkness recoiling about the sad tables, over the lonely night people.

The boy stood staring hungrily before him. He stood waiting to hear his name shouted, repeated, stood unmoving, waiting.

But there was only scattered dull automatic applause, already fading . . . faded.

The murmuring again, and the sound of the painted women moving tiredly from table to table, finally the music beginning again, and a few of the shadows at the tables, the thin young women and the drunken lonely men, rose, beginning their slow shuffling movements on the floor, swaying from side to side in the imitation of a dance, shadows within shadows. A harsh nasal voice was issuing from the large purple mouth of the woman swaying her fleshy spent body, singing slurring words.

Still, the boy did not move. He waited for the applause. Nothing. Nothing. Still he stood facing the twisting gray shadows. And still nothing.

Still no applause.

It would come, must come. The gray shadows of those people would recoil into the dark, the nasal voice would fade into thundering applause. He waited.

Nothing.

The trumpet blared, the voice of the woman cracked, the dancers moved like tangled puppets.

Suddenly, the boy was pushing at the hated people, making his way through the shadows, rushing through the small corridor, up the wooden steps, up into the small filthy room.

Frantically he opened the door.

The darkness, perfect, embracing, sprang upon him roaring as it swirled about him

He closed his eyes, leaning against the door, as if by doing so he could keep the sounds from reaching him, the murmuring, the nasal voice, the groaning trumpet. He was carried in a sea of motion, of motion and . . . silent applause.

As he whirled about the room sobbing, he groped above him for the light bulb. Darkness fled. The cheap room sprang into being, driving away the magic. The bulb shed its feeble light into every cobwebbed corner, every cracked piece of rotting wall.

And the boy stood staring about him, no longer sobbing, holding in both hands the small crucifix tied about his neck with the dirty piece of string.

The sea of pure motion receded.

The yellowish mirror before him . . .

The applause, he thought.

The applause.

The mirror . . .

He leaned forward, his hands releasing the crucifix gently, rising, touching his face. He looked into the live mirror before him. He stared at the face there, the reflection, and he smiled, caressing himself, looking into the yearning eyes fixed upon themselves. He moved treasuring the moment, closer to the mirror, closer, closer, closer, and the lips parted now, ready to touch now, to kiss the reflection now, himself.

The applause, he thought.

His fingers tightened, came crashing in a fist against the mirror.

And the boy, terrified, saw his own image shattered into pieces.

The publication of Pablo! would not have been possible with-
out the initiative of Professor Francisco Lomelí of the Universi-
ty of California-Santa Barbara, who worked to rescue from
oblivion an important manuscript in the John Rechy archive.
After working as an acquisitions editor of sorts and negotiating
with Mr. Rechy for the book's publication by Arte Público
Press, Dr. Lomelí worked as a facilitator throughout the
process. In working on the text, Dr. Lomelí, as a leading liter-
ary critic, has recognized important stylistic characteristics and
themes that antecede many aspects of the literature in the
decades following the writing of Pablo!; Dr. Lomelí's close tex-
tual analysis indicates that Rechy is more closely related to the
Latin American Boom than had previously been appreciated.

Afterword

John Rechy's *Pablo!* Marks the Emergence of a Trailblazer

It is a rare occasion when we come across an established author's first finished novel which he has shelved for decades to avoid comparisons with his celebrated first novel. That occurred with John Rechy and his novel *City of Night*. He had kept his first finished novel, *Pablo!* (written when he was 18 years old), away from publication so that it would not be perceived as depending on the success of his first novel . . .

Such a discovery occurred in 2014 when Rechy was awarded the Luis Leal Literature Award at the University of California at Santa Barbara. At the ceremonial dinner in downtown Santa Barbara with a group of colleagues, he proceeded to describe a manuscript he has kept since 1949 as somewhat odd, different and somewhat obscure. One could tell he shared mixed feelings about it as a viable experiment in first facing the task of finding his literary voice and style. I immediately became intrigued and proposed to him the possibility of a critical edition to unearth such a mysterious work as one more indicator of his oeuvre. This is how I came across *Pablo!*, not knowing what to expect, but open to encountering new or unknown facets of his writings. Through the years Rechy attempted revisions but he never felt he had achieved a final draft.[1] Recovering this early manuscript was no small feat, accomplished in part thanks to his close collaboration in revisiting what he had written with the intent to finalize it so many decades ago. Returning to the manuscript was filled with some nostalgia by the author and some trepidation by the critic, because we were not certain with what final product we would culminate. We both agreed that somehow *Pablo!* needed to be resurrected to cross fictional borders as well as temporal ones.

John Rechy has had a long and distinguished career of reinventing himself as a writer of fiction and non-fiction, having tra-

---

[1]The original manuscript of *Pablo!* had been deposited in the special collections at Boston University, from where Rechy recalled it for final adjustments. While the manuscript used here faithfully reflects the original version of 1948-1949, I checked for typographical errors, inconsistencies, proposed other options, and he made other adjustments to be able to reach the final version.

versed a wide spectrum of topics, sensibilities and styles. He is well known for his audacious and intrepid outlook in exploring sensitive issues unlike other American writers. Praise for his writing has come from various quarters, such as from Gore Vidal, who described him as "One of the few original American writers of the last century."[2] In another occasion in 1963, James Baldwin said in a letter to Grove Press editor Richard Seaver written shortly after his most recognized novel, *City of Night*, now an American classic, was published: "Rechy is the most arresting young writer I've read in a long time. His tone rings absolutely true . . . and he has the kind of discipline which allows him a rare and beautiful recklessness."[3] As such, he stands out as one of the most readily identifiable in the field of Chicano literature even though, ironically, some critics in the 1970s quibbled about his place in such a literary circle. Rechy prides himself in being recognized as a Chicano writer:[4] not someone who writes only "Chicano" literature but as a Chicano who writes about a wide range of subjects that deal with conflicting aspects of the human spirit. He embodies a perfect example of a writer who has not been constrained by his ethnicity, but rather, lets his ethnicity enrich his writing.[5] His many awards and recognitions attest to a writer who has remained true to his art without compromising either craft or narrative substance. As a result he was the first novelist to receive PEN-USA's Lifetime

---

[2]The quotation is from a letter by Vidal to the publisher of Charles Casillo's . . . biography . . . *Outlaw: The Lives and Careers of John Rechy* (Los Angeles, Advocate Books, 2002). . . . The quotation appears on the book's front cover as well as on the jacket of Rechy's *About My Life and the Kept Woman: A Memoir* (New York, Grove Press, 2008)

[3]A copy of the rare letter is included in the 50th anniversary edition of *City of Night* (New York: . . . Grove Press, 2013), p. xi.

[4]His father, of Scottish background, was born in Mexico City and his mother was born in the City of Chihuahua, Mexico.

Achievement Award, ONE *Magazine's* Culture Hero Award, the
Publishing Triangle's William Whitehead Award for Lifetime
Achievement, and a fellowship from the National Endowment
for the Arts.

He published his first short story, "Mardi Gras," in 1957 in
Evergreen Review, but he became an overnight sensation at 32
with the publication of *City of Night* in 1963, which reached the
national best-seller list over six months with eventual transla-
tions into over 20 languages. His many books and short stories
have received high acclaim because they tend to hit a sensitive
cord in mostly unexplored topics. But it was *City of Night* that
launched him definitively into the vanguard of American literature for unveiling the life of a male street hustler, creating in the
process a uniquely American picaresque narrator. The existen-
tialist protagonist embodies postmodernity through alienation
and disillusionment about the kind of life he can navigate in
multiple urban spaces. Among his other works are the following: *Numbers* (1967), *This Day's Death* (1969), *The Vampires*
(1971), *The Fourth Angel* (1973), *The Sexual Outlaw: A Documentary* (1977), *Rushes* (1979), *Bodies and Souls* (1983), *Marilyn's
Daughter* (1988), *The Miraculous Day of Amalia Gómez* (1991), *Our
Lady of Babylon* (1996), *The Coming of the Night* (1999), *The Life*

---

[5]Some Chicano critics, particularly during the cultural nationalist days of the
Chicano Movement of the 1970s, resisted including him within Chicano let-
ters because the principal agenda required positive depictions of protago-
nists, culture and family, but to address sexuality was still a taboo. It was an
era when negative representations were being revamped as an attempt to
compensate for past stereotypes, limitations and discrimination. But Rechy
preceded this trend by publishing his famous work in 1963 at a time when
most Chicanos and non-Chicanos had no idea of Chicano literary models.
At the same time he defies any facile or narrow classification that tries to
pigeonhole him because he covers a wide gamut of experiences, styles and
themes.

and *Adventures of Lyle Clemens* (2003), *Beneath the Skin: The Collected Essays of John Rechy* (2004) and *About My Life and the Kept Woman: A Memoir* (2008).

Much of his fiction depicts social outcasts who are on the fringe or in the underside of urban environments, generally lost and sustained by immediate gratification. In the process, segments of American urban experience unfold like conveyer belts of relegated lives while exposing the alienating effects on the individual. According to Terry Southern, Rechy's writings correspond to what he terms, "the self-revelatory school of Romantic Agony,"[6] that is, a poetics of tormented or troubled souls in search of a place to which they belong. They search for redemption, including self-fulfillment, but usually only encounter angst and negation. His daring thematics uncover specific social taboos, such as a gay hustler lifestyle that remained either outside the radar of the mainstream or overlooked explicitly in the annals of American literature. The subtlety, depth and complexity with which he delves into such topics cannot be denied or under-estimated and, yet, they could only resurface when times were more propitious and fertile. His cutting-edge audacity and acuity, in such works as *City of Night*, *Numbers*, *The Sexual Outlaw: A Documentary* and others, opened new ground by revealing characters that lived unorthodox, illicit or unconventional lives, as mainstream would have it. But it must be reaffirmed: Rechy both encapsulates and transcends such characters because he depicts the gravity of feelings and desires while searching for the self in others; and at the same time he faces their inadequacies and recalls his family niche paradoxically as anchor and perdition. This is why *City of Night* made such an impact, precisely

---

[6]See his article "Rechy and Gover," in *Contemporary American Novelists*, ed. Harry T. Moore (Carbondale and Edwardsville: Southern Illinois University Press, 1964), p. 225.

because it slammed the door open at the same time that its underground overtones permeated the narrative on a topic that could no longer be repressed or contained. The topic of sexuality and its variant lives had come of age as it deserved closer examination and greater scrutiny as a hushed reality that fled out of the closet. His groundbreaking fiction was instrumental in rendering these thematic concerns a seriousness and attention that few could adequately capture. He has approached such subjects with a most unique authenticity without compromising their complexities and multivalent renditions.

The work we recover here for the first time in this critical edition, titled *Pablo!*, stands out for its mature earnestness when he was merely 18 years old. It is also distinguishable for its many differences, as well as similarities, with his other known works. Its main distinction is twofold: as his first novel manuscript[7] it was consigned to a shelf for decades; and it explores Mayan myths and legends through a narrative approach ahead of its time. Readers will no doubt find new topics and a narrative world unlike his better-known novels. *Pablo!* expands and even challenges what we generally know about his other writings. This work in particular does not seem to fit his pattern of writing on the surface; yet, a closer examination will reveal that it is consistent with much of his later literary production, even in theme.

Pablo! is a rare novel for its distinctive strangeness and novelty, including its experimental contexture and stylistic innovations, thanks in great part to a gallery of archetypal characters (the man, the girl, the woman, the boy, etc.). Pablo—whose name is mentioned once near the end of the novel—emerges as the implicit protagonist. The work does not appear to have literary

---

[7]Rechy drafted two other novels before *Pablo!*—the first titled "Time on Wings," a historical novel, and "Bitter Roots," a semi- autobiographical novel, both of which were subsequently destroyed by him.

antecedents or a literary lineage within American literature at the time it was composed because Rechy creates an indigenous world of inferences and ambiguities. An exasperating jungle heat reigns in the narrative where Mayan Indian beliefs and rituals unfold, suggesting an ambience of a story translated, transcribed or written in another language of cryptic codes that do not pertain to English language conventionalisms. At times, the manuscript resembles the Mayan book of wisdom known as the *Popol Vuh*,[8] generally regarded as a book of counsel or a book of the people that recounts the cosmology of Mesoamerica. Other times, it reads like a fantasy, a fable, a legend or a parable with both mythic and folkloric ruminations that take place in an anonymous village "far away." This is consistent with the unspecific metaphorical elements within the *Popol Vuh*, an indigenous story of genesis and a subject of considerable controversy and speculation as to its veracity and originality. *Pablo!* shares some of its narrative tone with this classic pre-Columbian work through storyline, metaphors, rituals and even syntax, although John Rechy admits to not having read it, which makes it that much more remarkable. Many of the anecdotes resemble each other thanks to the non-linearity of the stories, including numerous anthropomorphic characters from nature (i.e. snakes and agoutis) that speak or acquire some protagonism. Echoes of an indigenous storytelling logic permeate the work through par-

---

[8]The oldest surviving manuscript of such a work is from 1701, written by the hand of Francisco Ximénez in Guatemala. It is presently archived at the Newberry Library in Chicago. Although data regarding its origins are somewhat vague and speculative, it nonetheless represents as a significant pre-Columbian document that is believed to reflect, although not in its entirety, the worldview of the Mayans through a series of codex-like texts that evolved much like a palimpsest. Scholars tend to respect the spirit of the manuscript, but not its overall composition due to possible contaminations and borrowings from Christian texts. Either way, it is considered to be the closest to an "original" Mesoamerican codex.

allels, déjà vus and apparent reincarnations, including witches that instigate violence and other inexplicable events. The *Popol Vuh* has dominated Central American literary and cultural aesthetics since time immemorial, so it is no coincidence that some of its aura and narrativity would reappear in Rechy's text—through osmosis or genius—upon indulging in the jungles of an atemporal Yucatán where the fantastic can seem real and time has stopped.

Pablo! stands out as a perplexing novel within American literature, particularly at the time it was composed between 1948 and 1949. It is more *sui generis* than a descendant, but its poetic affiliation with a later work by Peruvian written José María Arguedas, titled *Los ríos profundos* (1967), cannot be ignored for the coincidences on how it organically privileges myth and legend in Latin America. The coincidences are even more striking with Nobel Prize winner Miguel Angel Asturias' *Hombres de maíz* (1949) which was published the same year that *Pablo!* was written. Rechy's manuscript shares—more through poetic coincidence than anything else—similar qualities: a heavy reliance and presence of indigenous myth; the validation of native stories that seem to repeat themselves and extraordinary happenings that defy traditional realism. That is, the cyclical qualities of time as well as the mysterious characters connote phantom-like qualities in *Pablo!*, except that Rechy's work was written independently of the herein mentioned Latin American works. Can we surmise a prophetic literary bent on the style that would become greatly popularized in the novels of the Latin American Boom years later? Perhaps Rechy was onto something that no one else in the U.S. or Latin America had fully fleshed out or even intimated yet. Either way, his novel is highly intuitive and enigmatic about what it tells and how it accomplishes that. He definitely implies that the power of myth and legend is the main generator of action without completely giving into mythological determinism.

Rechy's novel refashions the myth of uniting the sun and the moon in a game of love, enacted by a series of archetypal characters that are anonymous, except for Pablo who screams out his name only once near the end. In a direct way, he defies his anonymity while challenging what a Mayan myth dictates: "... the soul must wander aimlessly until the sun and the moon shall fuse."[9] But his defiance is not enough. Much of the narrative is driven by an unrealized, obsessive desire, sometimes unrequited love, between the girl and the boy (Pablo), or the man and the woman, who represent archetypal embodiments lacking individuality precisely because they express groupings much within Joseph Campbell's concepts espoused in *The Hero of a Thousand Faces* (1949). Characters tend to be truncated sentimentally, isolated in their feelings and in search of an encounter with their respective partner, much as we might imagine the sun and moon seeking each other in a duel of love before disappearing in the sky. The subtheme of wandering aimlessly in search of close relationships repeats itself over and over, but more through subtle ruminations than explicit plotlines, thus underscoring the isolation and solitude that they share. In this regard, the novel resembles what Didier T. Jaén has noted to be a common denominator in Rechy's novels: the predominance of parables of lost salvation.[10] Here, it is more redemption in terms of lost love and untimely connections. Other times, the characters suggest a morality play with a lugubrious or ominous overtone while "souls of the unresting dead" roam the world. Death permeates the novel, hovering over all characters like a fog or the jungle heat. Escaping such an environment

---

[9]The quote on the legend appears as the novel's epigraph.

[10]"John Rechy," in *Dictionary of Literary Biography: Chicano Writers; Second Series*, Vol. 122, editors Francisco A. Lomelí and Carl R. Shirley (Detroit: A Bruccoli Clark Layman Book/Gale Research Inc., 1992), Pp. 212-219.

is not much of an option because their fate has been foretold, and they are simply re-enacting what is already known. All this would seem to be dictated by the stars or by Mayan myth. But Rechy has other ideas for Pablo.

The novel also contains various instances of magical realism, which should be considered quite ahead of its time for the late 1940s. For example, a girl is converted into a Tzacam flower, women are at times possessed in uncontrollable raptures, the moon's personification is accepted as something natural or real, popular fears circumvent characters' actions (i.e. the sin of a woman's unfaithfulness and the belief that a child suckling would pass down evil), a headless woman who is the mythological "Pol," a weeping Mother of Sorrows, and instances of witchcraft spells and trances. Again, morality and didacticism prevail by also revealing taboos of temptation in the form of rape and the obsessive pursuit of the Girl for the Boy of the "lithe body and the desperate eyes." As a prophetic witch states, "evil can enter the good and contaminate the heart" (p. 37). Most of the archetypal characters serve out predestined roles, but Pablo is the only one who defies such a framework, partly due to his incessant search of going beyond his town or transcending his domain. In a real sense, the omniscient narrator—who sometimes defers to a speaking voice of an unborn child, animals acting out as humans or other characters manifesting themselves—plays out a Pirandellian axiom in search of a protagonist through most of the novel; that is, until Pablo takes center stage dancing when he shouts his name, becoming in the process the only name in the entire work. He breaks the cyclical stranglehold of myth in that he claims individuality and free will. At that point, the novel takes on a character of defiance or the suspense of mythic disbelief.

From this point forward the novel becomes a detour of what it had been. If some characters had expressed themselves via internal monologues in a chorus of hushed voices, Pablo suddenly breaks that kind of collective paralysis. If others do not wish to expose themselves, due to vulnerability and possible reprisals, our protagonist becomes the brave soul to dare to speak his mind and desire openly. By declaring his wish to become a dancer, he assumes, for the first time a public face and agency aside from self-confidence. The more he dances, the more he acquires confidence and resoluteness about his new role, thus affirming a sense of presumption and vanity. At this point Pablo emerges from the leveling contours of sameness among the other characters, which explains in great part why he is the only character to acquire a personal name. His favorite activity in front of admiring mirrors becomes his vehicle to overcome indistinguishability and to realize his desires.

Near the end the tone of the novel changes radically: Pablo achieves an illusory moment of self-individuation, a new level of consciousness and freedom of expression while, at the same time, being unable to unite with the girl. He identifies his own salvation[11] within this world of control and sameness, but he still feels the pull from the girl who shines like the moon. Thus, Pablo repeats the myth of irreconcilability—including mythic determinism—with the girl who is the embodiment of the moon. The title of *Pablo!* with an exclamation mark is not gratuitous on the part of the author, but rather a heightened moment of demanding recognition.[12] Rechy has once again carved out a pattern for redemption and deliverance.

---

[11]A few pages earlier, a young man comments to the girl: "there is no substitute for salvation? no god for the damned?" (p. 136).

[12]Rechy indicated, in a personal email (March 29, 2014), that his intention at the point when his character shouts out his own name—as well as in the title—was to grant to his character the exclamatory recognition he has longed for in the novel.

Rechy's *Pablo!* offers an elusive, illusive and enigmatic narrative full of connotations that seem very contemporary even if it was written in 1949. His uncertainty about what the manuscript could contribute at that time caused him to stow it for decades. Now we can better appreciate its originality and boldness as a story of both redemption and choices because Pablo repels the advances of the girl who relentlessly desires him. The timeless narrative bound within a mythic present defies the traditional myth of predetermined love. The subtleties of the novel cannot be ignored because John Rechy proceeded from this time forward to pursue such a central theme in his subsequent works by contemporizing and situating such a topic in the large metropolitan cities. In that sense, *Pablo!* represents the seed that contains his poetics of searching for authenticity, acceptance and belonging.

Francisco A. Lomelí
University of California,
Santa Barbara

Bibliography

Casillo, Charles. *Outlaw: The Lives and Careers of John Rechy.* Los Angeles: Advocate Books, 2002.

Jaén, Didier T. "John Rechy." In *Dictionary of Literary Biography: Chicano Writers; Second Series*, eds. Francisco A. Lomelí and Carl R. Shirley. Detroit: A Bruccoli Clark Layman Book/Gale Research Inc., 1992. Pp. 212-219.

Popol Vuh: Literal Poetic Version: Translation and Transcription. Translator J. Allen. Norman: University of Oklahoma Press, 1964.

Rechy, John. *About My Life and the Kept Woman: A Memoir.* New York: Grove Press, 2008.

___. *City of Night.* The 50th Anniversary Edition. New York: Grove Press, 2013.

___. Unpublished Manuscript of "Pablo!" Provided by the author.

Southern, Terry. "Rechy and Gover. In *Contemporary American Novelists*, ed. Harry T. Moore.

Carbondale & Edwardsville: Southern Illinois University Press, 1964. Pp. 222-227.

Also By John Rechy

Novels:

City of Night
Numbers
This Day's Death
The Vampires
The Fourth Angel
Rushes
Bodies and Souls
Marilyn's Daughter
Our Lady of Babylon
The Miraculous Day of Amalia Gómez
The Coming of the Night
The Life and Adventures of Lyle Clemens
After the Blue Hour

Non-Fiction:

The Sexual Outlaw: A Documentary
Beneath the Skin: The Collected Essays
About My Life and the Kept Woman: A Memoir

Plays:

Rushes
Tigers Wild
Momma As She Became—But Not As She Was (one act)